UNCLE JACOB'S GHOST STORY

UNCLE JACOB'S GHOST STORY

DONN KUSHNER

HOLT, RINEHART AND WINSTON
New York

First published in the United States in 1986 by
Holt, Rinehart and Winston, 383 Madison Avenue,
New York, New York 10017.

Library of Congress Cataloging in Publication Data
Kushner, Donn.
Uncle Jacob's ghost story.
Summary: Paul discovers the story of his Great
Uncle Jacob, the black sheep of the family, who
believed that the ghosts of two beloved friends
followed him when he emigrated from Poland to America.
[1. Ghosts—Fiction.   2. Uncles—Fiction.
3. Jews—Fiction.   4. Emigration and immigration—
Fiction]   I. Title.
PZ7.K964Un   1986   [Fic]   85-14124
ISBN: 0-03-006502-X

First American Edition

Printed in the United States of America
1   3   5   7   9   10   8   6   4   2

ISBN 0-03-006502-X

To
NATHAN AND BENJAMIN

UNCLE JACOB'S GHOST STORY

1

N̲o one had a good word for Great Uncle Jacob. "He was a lazy, impractical person," Uncle Mordecai said. "Like the hippies these days, but that was years ago. A person like that in *our* family! I don't know where you heard of him."

Paul wasn't sure either. Jacob's was one of those names he had always known, like that of Loopy, his tattered cloth giraffe, whose long neck still hung over the "Wonders of Science" series on his bookshelf.

Uncle Mordecai kept looking down the street for the bus, though Paul knew it would only come into sight in five minutes. Uncle Mordecai said, "My father, your great uncle, was the middle one of seven boys. All the rest of them did well. Jacob was his older brother, by his father's first wife, who died. He lived in another village, in the old country." Uncle Mordecai's breath smelled like old cigars. "Do you understand all that?"

"Yes," Paul said, nodding as wisely as he could.

"Sure you do; it's family." Uncle Mordecai looked at Paul's face. "Well, what else do you want to know? I never met Jacob. He stayed behind at first, when his brothers came to America. He shouldn't have come at all: a completely impractical person. He never had to meet a payroll!"

"What happened to him, Uncle Mordecai?" Paul asked.

"Who knows? Where's that bus? I have to take you home and get back to the store."

Paul almost said that he didn't need anyone to take him home, that he could go on the bus alone. But then, he knew, Uncle Mordecai would start to worry and would phone his mother about the responsibility, in case something happened. He decided not to argue. The bus came round the corner, right on time, and Uncle Mordecai said quickly, "Forget what I said about Jacob, that he shouldn't have come. He had as much right to come over as anyone. But he was no credit to the family!"

Aunt Sophie used to tell Paul, "I live behind bars." It was her only joke; after she said it, she always added, ". . . and I'm glad to be there." Her apartment complex was surrounded by a high fence of sharp twisted iron bars. Many apartment buildings were protected this way now, but hers had been one of the first. The gate opened on a signal from her car. Paul used to think it was magic, until he learned about radio waves. Aunt Sophie told him they changed the signal every few weeks to keep bad people from discovering it and breaking in.

Now Aunt Sophie pursed her lips, as if she had seen a dirty spoon. "Uncle Jacob?" she said. "Why are you so interested? You shouldn't ask about him. Where did you hear his name, in your Aunt Bessie's house? He was a scoffer, a mocker; he believed in nothing! He went his own way. No one knew what he wanted. He was always asking questions. He made the family uncomfortable. We haven't talked about him in years!"

"But what happened to him?" Paul asked.

"He just disappeared. That's what happens to people who know more than anyone else." Aunt Sophie shook her head so strongly that the gold beads on her brooch jingled together. Then she saw the expression on Paul's face. He knew that his mother had just been telling Aunt Sophie about his report card. "Of course, you have to learn what they teach you in school," she added. "School's different."

Aunt Bessie wore a wide, pointed straw hat in the garden, like the poor Vietnamese peasants. "I pull off the little buds to make the rest of the plant straight," she explained. "Uncle Jacob?" she said thoughtfully. "I'll bet you saw his picture on your grandpa's wall. The family disgrace!"

Aunt Bessie was Paul's mother's older sister, but still might have got married if she wasn't so critical, the rest of the family said. They seemed to worry more about Aunt Bessie not being married than she did. "I suspect poor Jacob was an idealist, a dreamer," she said. "He was probably searching for his own kind of truth."

Paul had thought truth was when you didn't tell lies. "How many kinds of truth are there?" he asked.

"Too many." Aunt Bessie dug the dirt with a little hand shovel. "Almost divided you, you rascal!" She lifted out a long red worm. "We'll put him here so he doesn't get hurt."

"But what kind of truth did Uncle Jacob find?"

"*I* don't know. No one knows what he found. In fact"—she wrinkled her forehead — "no one knows what happened to him. Your grandpa might know, but you mustn't make him tired with too many questions."

Aunt Bessie mentioned this again a few days later: "If your grandpa looks tired, don't keep pushing him for answers." Paul and his mother were in Aunt Bessie's station wagon. After they left him at the Home where Grandfather lived, in New Jersey, west of the Palisades, the two sisters were going to a country auction. "We'll be back right after lunch," Paul's mother said, "so we can have a visit too. I hope you won't be bored."

"Why should he be bored?" Aunt Bessie said. "Don't wear your grandpa out. Make your notes so you'll remember, then you won't have to ask him more than once." She winked in the mirror.

Aunt Bessie was teasing Paul because the teacher in his special English class had told them to take notes before doing their essays. But when Aunt Bessie saw him writing in a small book about the posters on her wall and the pictures of the starving African children, she stopped him. "Don't act like a little police informer," she said. "Keep the notes in your head; that's the best place for them."

Grandfather shared a room in the Home with Mr. Eisbein. Mr. Eisbein had brown and blue spots on his skin. Grandfather's cheeks were clear and rosy; he had a small white bristly beard. Mr. Eisbein always talked first and most. "That's the one you were mentioning, Sam?" he asked. "The one with the newspaper stand on Times Square?"

"That's right, my half-brother Jacob," Grandfather said. "I just started thinking about that old story again the other day."

"The one who saw ghosts," Mr. Eisbein said.

"Ghosts?" Paul asked. Mr. Eisbein was always teasing. Paul didn't believe in ghosts, of course, any more than he believed in Santa Claus or the Prophet Elijah at Passover. But Mr. Eisbein was serious this time, very matter-of-fact. Paul glanced at the cupboard's dark curtains, in case something was hiding behind them.

"You'll frighten the boy, Abe," Grandfather said.

Mr. Eisbein said, "Not scary ghosts."

Paul was disappointed; what was the use of a ghost that didn't frighten you? "Not scary?"

"Not the kind with sheets and bones. We didn't have those in the old country. People's spirits didn't really like their bodies. Folks lived too close together, ten in a room sometimes. Just a shed in the back for a toilet, no bathtubs in the house."

"No bathtubs?" Paul grinned.

"You wouldn't have liked it. There was a bathhouse in the village; you went there once a week, if you were rich. There were bugs too, and fleas."

4

Paul shivered and scratched himself. "Take it easy, Abe," Grandfather said.

"I'm only explaining. People were still cheerful, but if their spirits had to hang around for any reason, they wouldn't take their bodies with them. The spirits might appear in dreams. Sometimes you thought you heard them, as voices in the wind."

"Brr," said Paul.

"You're not really frightened?" Mr. Eisbein asked.

"A little," Paul admitted. He took Grandfather's warm hand, something he wouldn't have done if his mother had been there.

But then, Grandfather wouldn't have spoken of ghosts at all if his mother had been there. She seemed to think Paul shouldn't even be told that people died. Two visits ago he had asked Grandfather about the empty room across the hall. Grandfather, who still had dried tears on his cheeks, started to say, "Poor Mr. Rappaport went so suddenly," when Paul's mother interrupted.

"He had to visit his relatives, didn't he?" she said, and shook her head in a way that she thought Paul didn't notice, until Grandfather changed the subject.

Grandfather squeezed Paul's hand. Then he said, casually, "Sometimes the spirit would enter another body."

"What we called a *dybbuk*," Mr. Eisbein added immediately. "But, of course, there would be a spirit there already. This could lead to no end of confusion. But your Great-Uncle Jacob's ghosts were something different again."

Grandfather smiled. "Yes, they were. Look, here is Uncle Jacob."

Behind his dresser Grandfather had a wonderful collection of old photographs; some were dull black and white, some were faded brown and yellow. There were fat men with bowler hats, and thin, bearded men with skullcaps or peaked caps. There were ladies with hair curled round their heads like fancy pastry, and there was a thin-faced lady with wispy hair and great dark eyes. All the faces looked serious, as if they had accomplished something just by having their pictures taken.

All but one: a small young man with a gentle, twisted face and a kind smile, who wore neither beard nor hat. He had his hand on his chin, as if he were keeping his face from smiling more. "That's Jacob," Grandfather said. He saw how Paul was staring at the picture and cleared his throat. "But the others were important people. Your Great-Uncle Max owned the biggest shoe store in Lublin. Sonja here was a rabbi's daughter and a scholar in her own right: she translated *Tom Sawyer* into Romanian. Your second cousin two times removed, Meyer," — this was the tall, thin man with melancholy spectacles — "worked himself up to be alderman in Lowell, Massachusetts. Howard made money on the New York Stock Exchange. A hospital wing is named after him. And Ruth and Eleazar . . ." Grandfather pointed to a serious middle-aged couple, each in a thick dark coat with a large cloth star attached. They were standing in the snow before the window of a fancy restaurant. Happy couples sat over coffee inside, and a stern waiter looked out onto the street. "They once owned a famous restaurant in Warsaw," Grandfather said.

Paul looked politely at all the pictures. "What about Uncle Jacob?"

"Well, what about Jacob?" Grandfather asked. "He came over to the New World. What should I tell you about him?"

"We know a lot," Mr. Eisbein said.

"We do," Grandfather admitted. "But you seem to know more than I do. Why is that?"

There was a pause. "It's because of the traveling salesmen," Mr. Eisbein said at last.

"Was Uncle Jacob a traveling salesman?" Paul asked.

"Hardly," Mr. Eisbein answered dryly. "He would have starved. But *I* was a traveling salesman—over the Five Boroughs, and out to the tip of Long Island. And before *that* I was a peddler upstate. I carried a pack between farmhouses. I walked twenty miles a day. On those long lanes, I felt that my pack had grown right onto me." His eyes measured Paul. "Why, boys your size on the way to school would touch my pack as if it were a hump. What's the matter?" he asked Paul. "Didn't you know that people used to touch a man's hump for luck? Did you ever see a hunchback?"

Paul shook his head. "I could show you a couple here," Mr. Eisbein said.

"Never mind," Grandfather said.

"The farm wives would be waiting for me, sometimes with a jug of milk." Mr. Eisbein licked his lips. "I'd make a sale here and a sale there: thread, pins, heavy iron pots and pans—those I sold first, if I was lucky. We knew everything," he added.

"Sure!" Paul exclaimed. Grandfather looked skeptical too.

"It seemed that way," Mr. Eisbein said. "Everyone wanted to talk to a stranger from the city. In the evening, at the country hotels, I'd meet other peddlers. We'd exchange stories."

"Business tips?" Grandfather asked.

"Those too. If a boy came home from college or from sea, all the peddlers knew. They'd swarm to the place: people would be buying then. Or, if a man escaped from prison and hid out on his family farm, we knew; we'd keep him supplied. We never told the police."

Mr. Eisbein rose from his chair by the window and opened a dresser drawer. He took out a cigarette, looked at it, and sadly put it back. "Not time yet," he said to Grandfather.

"We even learned about murders before the police did," he added.

Paul asked quickly, "Did Uncle Jacob murder anyone?"

Mr. Eisbein gave him a look. "What a question! He wouldn't step on a cockroach!" He went back to his own story. "On one farm, an old man killed his wife; he buried her behind the barn. A peddler saw him, a warty man named Kropnick; others began journeying miles to see the secret grave. When he was arrested we wondered whether we had set the police on him. Was it this line of sad-eyed men with packs that made them suspicious? No, he gave himself up, through remorse. The day he was hanged, no peddler would set out on his route, as if we had all lost a brother."

Grandfather asked, "Did his spirit walk?"

"Probably not. It didn't have enough interest in life to come back," Mr. Eisbein replied. "If it had, we would have known.

"When we peddlers came to the city and began to specialize," he continued, "we shared our secrets in soda fountains and saloons. If a despairing grocer burned his shop for insurance, we knew. We asked each other, 'What did he think? Who did he speak to? When did he decide to strike the match?' As if his thoughts were our own."

"Did Uncle Jacob burn down his store?" Paul slipped in.

Mr. Eisbein shook his head strongly. "He was no more an arsonist than he was a murderer!" Then his voice softened. "He had a newsstand, one of those stands which were like private post offices where people left messages for each other. We would say, 'Have you seen so-and-so? His brother sent him a desperate letter.'

"But your Uncle Jacob's newsstand was something special, and what happened there was even more so. I knew him; recently, I've thought of him more and more. At one time his story went round all the traveling salesmen in New York City."

"You know only part of the story, Abe," Grandfather said. "You know about it in New York; I know about it in the old country."

"Even there, I could probably add a few details," Mr. Eisbein said.

Paul was afraid his mother would return before he had heard Uncle Jacob's story, but while they were having lunch in the dining room, she telephoned. Aunt Bessie had learned of a second auction which she just had to attend. They would come for Paul a little later, certainly before dark.

Two ladies shared their table in the dining room: fat Mrs. Schwarz, who seemed so impressed Paul could read a newspaper that he didn't tell her he had already been doing so for five years, and Mrs. Dobin, a thin lady with very yellow hair who giggled at everything Mr. Eisbein said. Paul had thick curls which ladies usually liked to stroke, so he watched these two cautiously. But Mrs. Schwarz seemed too shy to touch him and

Mrs. Dobin was more interested in Mr. Eisbein. When they got up after dessert, she said, "I learned a new kind of gin rummy, just for you, Abe."

"Well . . ." Mr. Eisbein started to turn back from the door.

Grandfather cleared his throat. Paul said, "Come *on*, Grandpa." Grandfather followed him out of the door, and after a moment Mr. Eisbein came too.

Behind the Home was a narrow, very green park that extended to the river. It was pinned down on each side by a tall apartment building. Across the river, no wider here than the Thruway, were colorful fairgrounds, full of canvas tents and booths and great turning wheels. The air was so clear that all objects glowed with a light of their own.

Grandfather and Mr. Eisbein sat on a bench facing the river. At first, while they tried to settle who knew most about Uncle Jacob, Paul stood on the bank and skipped stones on the water. The first stone bounced three times, the second, two. Then the third stone seemed to take off on its own. It skipped ten times, almost across the river, toward the bandstand in the fairground, a round green iron structure with nine pillars.

In the bandstand two men and a woman were playing guitars. The melodies were strange but familiar. Though Paul could not name the tunes, he was sure he had heard them somewhere: they were like the country tunes from the radio of the house next door that he sometimes heard while falling asleep. The musicians started to sing, softly, but he could hear the words clearly as they traveled across the water:

> "Now I'll begin to tell you my story,
> Listen, while shadows pass over the river."

Then the voices faded, but the guitars continued, a measured strumming to introduce the story which the singers would soon tell.

Grandfather called; he was now ready to begin. Paul went and sat between him and Mr. Eisbein on the bench, very still.

2

Jacob (Grandfather said) was the last person anyone would have expected even to see a ghost, let alone become the close acquaintance of several. He was a small, active young man, as lively and curious as a kitten. When he heard a noise, he ran out to investigate it. If he heard people talking, his ears pricked up, and only his good manners kept him from actually eavesdropping. If an idea made it to his little town across the swamps, the dense forests, the ignorant, starving farms, he picked it up immediately. Still, he chewed on it a long time before deciding how much he wanted to swallow and digest. He loved the beautiful, shining products of the human mind, but he would accept nothing too easily. He considered himself a "rationalist"; that is, a person who believes in the power of reason. There should be, he thought, an explanation for everything: every event should have a natural, reasonable cause. (Grandfather winked at Paul. "He was just like you," he said.)

The village where he lived, Niekapowisko, somewhere in eastern Poland near the Russian border, was a strange place for a rationalist. If you looked at it from the low northern ridge of hills that shut it off from the outside world, you would see first the peasants' cottages, scattered among the fields without apparent reason like blocks flung from a child's hand, each cottage surrounded by its tangled garden of sunflowers. Close to the square church tower with its onion-shaped dome was a row of dirty yellow brick houses. The few village officials lived here, and the merchants, with their shops below and their apartments above. A thick, dark stand of fir trees behind the church made it seem, from a distance, as if the village ended there, but if you walked between the trees you would come to a group of old stone houses, clustered round a little pond.

Here the Jews of the village lived. They had settled more than a hundred years before: the nobleman who had owned the village had built a circle of fine stone houses for this group of hardworking artisans and merchants. He had gone bankrupt long since, and the houses were dry and crumbling. The steep, pointed roofs were thatched with straw that brushed the ground below their eaves and hung over their windows like eyebrows, beneath which the cloudy panes looked sadly at each other. Ghosts would have been right at home in such buildings. On the chimneys stood storks on one leg, looking at their fellows as if they were waiting for a signal to fly away together. Ducks paddled in the pond round a great rock that some drunken peasants had once thrown in, and that nobody had figured out how to remove.

Behind a willow whose branches dipped in the pond stood the inn, with three balconies and an iron roof. The innkeeper, who knew that talking made people thirsty, had set out trestle tables where his customers could chat with their friends, beneath the willow, near the seven busy market stalls.

Across the pond, past the houses, above a small wooded ravine was a squat building with a cylindrical copper cupola. This was the synagogue, built by the one wealthy member of the community before he took himself and his business to Warsaw. In the dusty square in front of it, their black coats flickering among the black trees, old men walked up and down discussing eternal laws and truths.

Jacob often sat before the inn and watched them. But don't think (Grandfather warned Paul, shaking his finger) that Jacob was a loafer or a wastrel. No, he had a decent job as agent and accountant for a wealthy gentile landowner, an able, eccentric man who never counted the hours his bright assistant kept so long as he did his work. Jacob never had so good an employer again. As he was quick and could concentrate till the job at hand was done, the young man had plenty of free time. He liked to wander alone in the forest with his thoughts, or to sit with his friends before the inn, making one mug of beer last a long time and watching the world go by.

Even in such a small place, things happened, people talked. Those at the market were especially interested in demons. The woman who sold fish heads, who had buried three husbands, said, "You should never aim too high. My first husband, may he rest in peace, wasn't satisfied with our well: he wanted a deeper one, lined with bricks too! I told him, demons haunt such wells, but he wouldn't listen. In one business after another he failed. He bought corn from the peasants that he couldn't sell; he made artificial flowers for the city, no luck there either. Finally, scrap metal and rags; this business went downhill too, and he went with it. I told my second husband to close the well, but *he* wouldn't listen. He was a peddler; one night, crossing a forest, he became lost in the snow. My third husband never listened to anything; he just wasted away before my eyes. How can people ignore such warnings?"

"You're right," said Fat Bella, who sold hot corn gruel. "Sensible people know the air is full of warnings. You can read signs in the way dogs howl, or cats whine; even in the way pigs squeal." She spat, then announced to the market at large, "I knew a wise woman who could interpret the flight of birds. She lived to be ninety-five. No one with sense would plan a piece of business without consulting her."

"What nonsense." Jacob laughed softly. "A superstitious person will find 'signs' everywhere. See, this willow branch has touched my shoulder." He put it aside. "I might tell you it means bad luck, say that the next business deal I recommend for my boss will fail. And as for the demons: the woman's poor husbands died of poverty, cold, sickness. Those are demons, if you like, but it is better to drive out such demons yourself by

12

making a better life." He smiled. "As they do in America!"

Jacob was sitting with his two best friends, Simon and Simon's sister, Esther. Simon was a pale young man, a head taller than Jacob; he always bent down to hear him speak when they discussed books together. At this moment his finger was holding open a translation of Shakespeare's plays. His dreamy eyes were gentle and trusting, as if he were sure the world was better than it appeared. Esther was shorter, strong and rosy, with great dark eyes. Her mouth was serious but always seemed as if it were about to smile.

"Yes, America," Jacob said. "There they know how to live: a great, free, hopeful nation. They are not bound by old men and superstition, as we are."

Now Esther did smile. "And are the streets there paved with gold, Jacob?"

"I know better than that, of course. Their history is dark enough, but it's such a big, open country. There, if you work hard, if you use your intelligence, you have a good chance for a useful, happy life. Why not? That should be the law everywhere. But in America such laws are often obeyed. There, when they have problems, they solve them: they solve them scientifically."

Jacob had been reading as much science as he could. He loved the laws of physics and chemistry that showed how particles and substances move and combine with each other. How thrilled he was when he learned of Newton's laws of motion and gravity! "Imagine," he said, "one of us discovered all that."

("One of us?" Mr. Eisbein asked. "He meant a human being," Grandfather explained. "Oh," Mr. Eisbein said.)

Lately, Jacob had found translations of the works of Darwin, books that showed the same kinds of laws applied to plants and animals, to all the living world. It all seemed beautiful and simple: he saw no reason why scientific methods should not also apply to human life.

And now Jacob began to talk about the laws of behavior that governed people, whether in America or here. "Look," he told his friends, "at Fertig, the beggar." He pointed at a tall, striking figure across the pond. Winter and summer, Fertig dressed in an old army greatcoat with the insignias torn away. He always kept his right hand over the left breast, where the medals had hung. His face was so thin, his nose so strong and curved, that on first view he resembled a great, fierce bird, and he asked for help proudly, as if *he* were conferring the favor.

"Fertig is a beggar. Fertig wants money," Jacob said. "Therefore, he will naturally approach a person who has money, rather than one who hasn't."

At that moment two men were walking round the pond from opposite directions. One was a tall, stocky man in a fine new coat, and boots that shone even through the dust. The other was short and meager, his ragged beard looking moth-eaten, his shoes more tattered than those of Fertig himself. Jacob waited confidently for the beggar to approach the prosperous man, who, with a good-natured smile, was already reaching into his waistcoat pocket. But Fertig ignored him and stationed himself before the short, ragged man, who immediately stopped and looked behind him as if the beggar must be addressing someone else.

"Your Excellency," said Fertig, bowing from his great height, "Out of your bounteous heart, help one who is less fortunate than you."

"Less fortunate than I?" the poor man said in amazement.

"Smitten by every stroke of ill chance," Fertig boasted.

"But I have children to feed," the man stammered.

"And I have none, only myself. Even my *needs* are less than yours."

"I have to work for every penny," the poor man said desperately.

"And how fortunate you are! Work brings dignity. *I* am forced to beg. Who would employ *me*?" Fertig bowed again, then straightened up with authority. The poor man, as if in a trance, hunted among his rags for a small coin. The beggar breathed on the coin, rubbed it to a glow on his sleeve, and bowed profoundly to his benefactor, who also began to look proud and upright. Then Fertig bowed again, but coldly and distantly, to the wealthy man, who all this time had kept his fingers in his pocket; he would certainly have given now, but the beggar stalked past him.

Simon looked down and his sister smiled, though kindly, at Jacob's embarrassment. After a moment, Jacob smiled too. He did not take himself seriously enough to mind when he was proved wrong. Besides, he was with the two people he loved best in the world. He had known Simon all his life — Esther too, though he and she had only recently started to notice each other; now they could hardly bear to look away.

As small boys, Jacob and Simon had splashed in the pond and built castles in its mud. Later, they had made little huts of branches in the forest, hidden from the peasant boys, who didn't like them.

("Why not?" Paul asked. Mr. Eisbein grunted. "Never mind," Grandfather said. "That's the way it was.")

They would spy on the farmers and sometimes even pick apples and plums; just a few, and mainly for the excitement and the danger. And it was dangerous: the farmers would gladly have set dogs on them, or stabbed them with pitchforks. The boys ate the fruit quickly so that their parents would never learn what they had done.

Most dangerous of all was fishing in the bend of the river by the soldiers' camp. They put their poles out between the reeds, and if a fish bit, pulled it up steadily to hide the movement. They could see the soldiers' red caps passing back and forth beyond the bushes on the opposite bank. They could hear their horses snorting and see the strong beasts caper. The soldiers, too, were like springy young animals, lively and dangerous. Their tight-fitting uniforms were decorated with belts, buckles, pockets. Their jaunty caps glowed in the sun. Sometimes they took off their jackets and shirts and leaped over the horses, with just a hand on the saddle. In the evening they would sing around the fire. Some played guitars or balalaikas; others danced, squatting down and shooting out their feet so rapidly that their bodies seemed magically suspended in air. But the finest sight of all was when a line of proud horses with their slim, upright riders trotted across the arched bridge, ready to ride off in an instant over the fields or, it seemed, through the sky itself. The boys could hardly keep their hands from clapping; they were ready to stand and cheer.

They never did. They had been warned that the soldiers didn't like strangers. And they themselves had once seen two old men stray into the camp. The soldiers made these old men dance by flicking their whips under their feet. Afterward the soldiers boasted that except for the first strokes, their whips had never actually touched the dancers. The soldiers laughed and poked each other in the ribs; the old men, they cried, with their beards flying in the air, their hands holding on to their broad hats, looked like crickets capering on hot stones.

("Why are you laughing?" Mr. Eisbein asked Paul. "You find it funny too, eh? Little Cossack!" Paul thought a moment. "No, I guess not." "Take it easy, Abe," Grandfather said. "The soldiers were like children too; they could be cruel without thinking about it.")

That time, the soldiers had finally let the old man go. But the boys remembered. Afterward, when Jacob spoke of America he would say, "There, where the soldiers don't make the old men dance."

Jacob certainly wanted to go to America. But it wasn't such a strange idea for a young man to want to go to America; I wanted to go myself (Grandfather said). Many of my friends wanted to go. This was at the end of the last century, and, as the years passed, the reasons for going became clearer to everyone. Two of my older brothers were already there. They worked to send for me; I went over and worked to send for the next ones. We hadn't forgotten Jacob. He would have his turn too — if he could wait that long.

He and his two friends were more eager to go than anyone else. Simon and Esther had their own special reason. They loved the stage: to them, an actor's life was the most glorious on earth. Where could they lead such a life better than in America?

They devoured any information they could find on the American theatre. They cut out fillers from the Polish newspapers. In junk shops in nearby towns, they bargained for old theatrical magazines. Parts of Broadway in New York City, they learned, had recently been lined with electric lights. In their own village only the police station and the railway depot had such glaring objects. The expression "The Great White Way" glowed in their minds. Simon and Esther were convinced that audiences in the Broadway theatres numbered in the thousands, all in new clothes, with clean faces that glimmered in the houselights. They thought of those endless rows of uplifted faces almost as pavements leading to heaven.

To them, the great actors in America were more than human. They read that the enchanting, elfin Maude Adams rode a private railway car right from the stage door to her country estate on a lake in Long Island. Richard Mansfield, aristocratic and aloof, also had his own country estate, his own railway car and yacht. Even Helena Modjeska, a Polish actress, had become a star in New York. There seemed to be room for everyone!

Meanwhile, Simon and Esther pursued the theatre as best they could. They saved their pennies for whatever fourth-rate traveling show passed through their village. They begged the stage managers for jobs as extras, as stagehands, as ushers. They offered to sweep the old stage floor, free, if they could watch the rehearsals.

They acted out their own plays, too. Simon, who was apprenticed to a tailor, saved remnants of cloth for costumes. People said that when they played a scene between Macbeth and Lady Macbeth in an open meadow, you felt that thick castle walls and drunken, murderous soldiers were all around you. When Esther played the ambitious wife of the fisherman in the old legend, you felt she really was capable of being the king, the emperor, and even the Pope himself!

Naturally, they concealed such plays from all but a few close friends, and they were especially careful that old Reb Nahum didn't see them. Many of the old men distrusted the theatre, as they did most worldly devices, but were too busy with the sweet intricacies of their studies to notice. Reb Nahum yearned to be a scholar but didn't have the brains. Instead, he had to content himself with spying out and condemning things he thought he understood.

At a performance by a traveling troupe of Molière's *Le Bourgeois Gentilhomme*, Reb Nahum mounted the stage and lectured the overworked actors about the vain lives they led. After that, the management barred him from the local theatre. But amateur theatricals by Jacob's friends were still fair game.

He tracked down a performance in a forest grove of the workmen's scene from *A Midsummer Night's Dream*, and shouted furiously, "Foolishness! Foolishness! Degradation and wickedness!" until the young people fled. Only one person, probably Esther, had the courage to hurl a clod of earth at him.

Simon and Esther hid their favorite play, which they had invented themselves, from almost everyone; they told only Jacob about it. In this play, Simon took the part of a good and powerful prince; Esther, that of a wandering princess who loved him but who could only marry him after he had brought complete justice to his kingdom. This might have been easy: the princess knew many magic words, each of which would right a specific wrong. But each word could be used on only one occasion, and she never knew in advance which words and wrongs fitted each other.

Though they acted this play out in public, they did so secretly. Simon wore a gold kerchief round his neck, beneath a high collar. Esther wore her best black shawl, with another shawl of gold silklike material hidden under it. Inside her high boots were thin gold-colored slippers. They had to circle round the person for whom the magic word was intended, but in a casual fashion, so that no one would know what they were doing.

Thus, when the orphan, Lisa, in her pretty white dress, strolled across the market toward Herschel, the tanner's son, Simon and Esther walked behind her, to one side and then to the other, and finally overtook her, while at each point of the compass Esther whispered the word "thingummy." This was to ensure that her dress would not be spattered with mud by any passing horse or running boy. And the spell worked: from the other side of the pond Simon and Esther saw Lisa talking shyly to the young tanner, swaying gently on her feet, as slim and white as a birch tree.

They once followed the fat peasant, Stanislas, who was taking a shortcut by the pond on his way home from the main village tavern. They hoped that the word "slivovitz" would make him sleep off the drink in his barn, instead of finding the energy to beat his children again. But this time they must have used the wrong word: from two streets away they soon heard the screams of children and the deep voice of Stanislas singing old hymns.

On other occasions they tried other words, and often it seemed that the words brought good luck. Simon and Esther almost believed that the words were magic, that it was really only a question of using the right one at the right time. But one day Esther appeared alone, close behind the postman in his gray uniform. This time her costume was not hidden. Her golden shawl was spread wide; she stepped through the mud in her golden slippers; a red leather belt with small bronze bells enclosed her waist. She circled the puzzled postman as he approached Jacob's house, repeating the word "mandrake"; then, as he approached her own house, the word "asafetida."

As the postman came to the door of each house, he had to make his way through a swarm of geese who swayed their long necks and hissed at him. But alas, neither Esther's words nor the hissing geese kept the evil away. The postman had been delivering the notices that told a young man whether he must become a soldier immediately or whether, for a while, he could stay home. In those days such matters were determined by chance in a central office in the capital. This time, Jacob and Simon had bad luck: the army claimed both of them.

And what a time they had (Grandfather said, and Mr. Eisbein nodded vigorously)! Better not to say too much about it. Jacob and Simon were trained by the methods of the day: curses, kicks, cold, dirt, and hunger. They could barely move in their

19

stiff uniforms. They carried great loads forever through the mud. Jacob almost forgot that man should be a rational being. He looked down at his clumsy boots, hidden in black mud, and could imagine no reason for his feet being there, let alone the rest of him. He and Simon were together at first, but soon he was sent east into Russia, almost to the Ural Mountains. Simon was sent north, near St. Petersburg as it was called then, a place where it never became dark in summer but where, to him, the sun showed nothing worth seeing.

Then the war, which had been snuffling round the horizon like some clumsy dragon, arrived with all its noise and smoke. What they call the Russo-Japanese War (Grandfather said): you probably haven't heard of it, but it was a big, important war. And Jacob, once he had been trained to walk with others in a straight line and so present a better target, was shipped across the biggest country in the world to fight the Japanese: small, tidy, fierce, disciplined men who didn't like foreigners and had a lesson to teach them. They taught it to the Russian army but good! They beat the great loutish soldiers and sent them all the way back again, scratching their beards and shaking the lice from their clothes. Jacob never found out what he had been doing there.

("But there is a story about him," Mr. Eisbein said. "When he first arrived at the front, his sergeant pointed out the direction to shoot. 'Are you crazy?' Jacob asked 'There are *people* out there!' " "That's an old one," said Grandfather. "I heard that story too. It wasn't about Jacob. It could have been about anyone." "Then it could have been about Jacob too," said Mr. Eisbein.)

But at least he came back unharmed (said Grandfather), with a whole skin and a whole spirit. He still looked around him; he was still curious about the landscape he could see between the slats of his crowded freight car. They passed over steppes, through mountains and plains, through the endless forests of Siberia, till it seemed he was one of the poor exiles sent away there for life. That's what they did with troublesome political prisoners in those days. Yet Jacob knew the journey would end; the thought that he would see his friends again made it both longer and shorter.

But his village had changed. The streets were empty, the shop windows boarded up; dead smoke hung in the air; the storks had flown from the rooftops. The first people he saw on the banks of the pond turned away, back to their houses, to avoid talking to him. At last his anxious questions brought him the terrible news: Simon and Esther were dead.

A sickness called typhus had struck the village. This disease comes when people are very dirty and crowded together, as in times of war or great poverty. Now we know what causes typhus, but then it seemed like just another evil visitation from heaven. People were even afraid to tend the sick, and left them to die alone. When Simon heard in his camp that Esther had caught the disease, he did a foolish, desperate thing. He deserted the army, took off his uniform, and returned to the village to help her. It was crazy: the penalty for desertion in time of war was death, and of course the soldiers could guess where he had gone. But when they came for him, he himself was sick. He and Esther died within a few minutes of each other.

("So that's what he did: he deserted. I remember now," Mr. Eisbein said. Paul thought about the word "deserted." He recalled a name that had been whispered round his house. "Was it like my cousin Sherman who went to Canada?" "Yes," said Mr. Eisbein. "No, it wasn't the same thing at all!" Grandfather said. "Sherman is a very foolish, very ungrateful young man!" Mr. Eisbein winked. "Of course, no one in his family had typhus," he said. "They certainly did not," said Grandfather. "People don't get typhus in this country!")

Others were gone too (Grandfather continued). Fertig the beggar was dead. Fat Bella, who read warnings everywhere, had not read her own accurately enough. Many of the old men who had spent all their time contemplating God's nature were now studying it closer to hand. The village was very quiet; the only sound in the circle of stone houses was the waves of the pond lapping against the great rock.

Jacob sought desperately for memories of his friends; he

21

closed his eyes in the forest glades where they had acted their plays, hoping against all reason for some message. He stood beside their graves. Nothing was there (Grandfather said. He looked at Paul's frightened, expectant face). Not a ghost, not a shadow, not a whisper. Jacob's friends might have never existed. Now there was nothing to keep him in the village. Jacob picked up some work from his old employer, saved all his money, sold what little he possessed, got a bit of help from his brothers who were already in America, and set off for America too.

3

æ

M r. Eisbein announced, "I have to go to the bathroom."
He stood up and massaged his left leg, which had fallen
asleep. "You tell him about the first years in America, Sam.
All these family chronicles; I don't find them interesting. But
you listen," he told Paul. "They're part of the story. The
ghosts come later; I'll be back by then." They watched him
walk away, bowing to a young woman who pushed a baby
carriage and to a girl reading on another bench.

"It's interesting enough," Grandfather called after him.
"Mr. Eisbein doesn't consider family matters important," he
explained. "His life took another direction."

Jacob's story began like that of so many others (Grandfather
said). He came over in steerage; that is, in a big dormitory in
the hold of a steamship. A hard trip, but he had been in worse
places. He wasn't even seasick; all the bumpy marches had
cured him. Only, he was unable to mix with those around
him. However close they were pressed together, he felt he was
standing alone. Sometimes the shadow of a face or the flash of
an eye reminded him of Esther or Simon, but when he turned
eagerly, it was always a stranger.

He saw the Statue of Liberty on a misty day, shining with drops of moisture, like a great piece of green candy. Someone met him at Ellis Island. His brothers had already found work; they had made contacts. A path was open to him, just the kind of path he had talked of so hopefully in the old country. But now, this no longer appealed to him: he was like a person who had been looking forward to a great feast but found, when he sat at the table, that he wasn't interested; he was still hungry, but he didn't want any of the dishes that were set before him.

("Did he want ghosts?" Paul asked, without knowing why. Grandfather looked at him keenly and curiously. "Not at that time," he said.)

Jacob found work first with his half-brother Hyman, Uncle Mordecai's father. Hyman was lucky: he had already fallen on his feet. A handsome man, a snappy dresser, very well spoken, he had just married a rich girl. That is, her father owned four candy stores, two on Staten Island, one in Brooklyn, one far away in Newark, New Jersey. Hyman had been given the one in Newark to manage. It was the busiest of all, on a crossroad near three schools, and he persuaded his father-in-law to give Jacob a job as his helper. He explained to Jacob that first he would have to watch the front of the store so that children didn't steal the candy. Hyman had a deadly fear of theft. He might make as much as one hundred dollars a day — and that was really a lot of money then — but if a child swiped even a gumdrop his whole evening turned sour. So he said Jacob should just sit by the front door and watch. Later, he would initiate him into the mysteries of the candy business.

After two days, Jacob quit. He explained the reasons patiently to Hyman, in the English that he was just beginning to pick up, and that Hyman insisted on speaking. First, Jacob said, he saw no real harm in the children: a piece of candy here or there was not theft — it was a game, such as he had once played. Second, he believed that a watchman would drive children away, both innocent and guilty. The potential losses were greater than the trifling amount saved, so the practice was bad for business. Third, he felt that even a simple person like himself had dignity, and to be posted to spy on children was an offence to this dignity. It might also be argued, he added, that too much candy was bad for children, but since he had accepted the job he could not raise this as a reason for watching or not watching. This was not why he was leaving now: he wanted to make this point quite clear.

Great-Uncle Hyman never got over the shock of having a new immigrant with a much stronger accent than his own tell him what was what. He later persuaded his father-in-law to sell his stores and deal in candy wholesale. In this business—which he followed with moderate success — Hyman hoped to avoid dealing with thieving children and such disturbing people as Jacob.

A cousin of a cousin with a chicken farm on Long Island offered Jacob a job next. The farm was small but very efficient: the cousin didn't believe in letting chickens run around to waste energy and catch diseases. They spent their lives in coops, in a dimly lighted henhouse, where they were disturbed as little as possible. Straw was put down for the laying hens and the eggs were removed through a special door. A calculation had been made of the most profitable time to kill the hens: a balance between egg production, food expenses, and tenderness of the flesh. Nowadays (Grandfather said) almost all chicken farms are run that way. The cousin — what was his name? I forget it — was years ahead of his time, and justly proud.

Jacob helped in all these operations. There was another helper too: the cousin's younger brother, Moishe, of whom the chicken farmer was by no means proud. Moishe was a fat, gentle, blue-eyed man with light blond hair that was always blowing over his face. He was, to be frank, not very bright. His brother had to bring him over to America: how could Moishe look after himself in the old country? But he often regretted this: what a pity, the cousin said, to uproot Moishe from the simple life in Poland and the air of quiet study that he had loved. Yes, Moishe had the instincts for meditation and scholarship, even though he could barely read, and could certainly not follow the involved Talmudic arguments.

Still, Moishe did think; perhaps he thought the more clearly for being slow. As he went about his chores or sat in the sun outside the henhouse, he would ponder on a verse from the Torah, trying in his simple way to get at its meaning. But he didn't neglect his work; he was good at tending chickens, kindly, thorough. He liked to see the birds eat and scratch in the clean straw. He took pride in the eggs they laid and admonished them to "be fruitful and multiply." When the chickens were killed, however, he became so upset that his brother began to send him away beforehand—but somehow he always knew.

When Jacob came, Moishe had been considering for some weeks the lines from Exodus: "But the more they afflicted them the more they multiplied and the more they spread abroad." These words, of course, described the situation of the Jews under Pharaoh, in Egypt, but Moishe saw a new meaning in them. He repeated them under his breath, thought deeply of them, and in the end decided that they also applied to the chickens. Then his feelings for these birds, with their mild, stupid heads, their short-sighted, jerky motions, became more important to him than his duties, more important than his fear of his brother. Moishe decided he should set the chickens free.

He explained all this to Jacob, who had grown fond of him. And Jacob, instead of trying to dissuade him — though that would have been difficult—or telling his brother, suggested to Moishe that the best time to open the henhouse was on Friday morning, when his brother usually went to the bank.

Why would he do this? As he explained later, he had begun to respect Moishe's slow powers of reasoning: Moishe went in the right direction, with no false turns due to intellectual vanity. Chickens were God's creatures too. Of course, in any hen yard the housewife would chase them for supper, but each had a chance to escape, and a chicken might even last till a ripe old age. Jacob had been more disturbed than he would admit by the scientific processing in this modern factory, in which no chicken tasted freedom, the fixed stages of life and death. Why shouldn't chickens have a chance too?

Jacob found an excuse to be absent on Friday morning, not to avoid responsibility, but because, as he explained later, he did not want to rob Moishe of any credit. A few market gardeners in that part of Long Island — it's mostly built up now, of course — still talk of the escape. Chickens, as free and fearless as in the first days of creation, wandered up and down the roads, into farmyards and gardens, even scratching on doors to be let in. Many were recaptured, others doubtless ended up in strange stewpots, but Jacob always liked to think that some of the birds had gone quite free.

Of course, his employer was furious! He had to keep his brother, but not Jacob, whom he held entirely responsible. When Jacob tried to discuss the moral basis of Moishe's arguments, the cousin accused him of impiety and blasphemy, of making a mockery of religion, of using a poor simpleton to distort the Holy Word.

Grandfather cleared his throat. "And this reputation followed him, especially after what happened between him and my brother Max, your Aunt Sophie's father. Max was the most pious one of all. He was a lumber dealer in Cincinnati. Jacob worked for him for a time. By then, his English was good and he had learned American accounting methods. There was a future for him in the company."

But Paul was only half listening. He was watching, on the riverbank, a row of green frogs, as shiny as those on the buffet at home. Each frog looked toward the fairgrounds, where sparse crowds now strolled among the booths. The singers on the bandstand walked round too, strumming their guitars gently. A subtle motion in the river attracted Paul's eyes again. A slim brown snake swam past the frogs in a dignified "S," as if its mind were on higher things.

Paul heard Grandfather's voice again. "Yes, they quarreled over Max's plan to put his name and his wife's and some verses in gold leaf on a window of the synagogue. The expense would stop him sending his daughter to college. Well, in those days people didn't think much of college for girls, though Sophie had her heart set on it then. You wouldn't get her to admit it now, of course. Sophie never forgave Jacob for criticizing her father's use of his own money!'' Grandfather shook his head.

"What are you talking about now? Have you got to the newsstand?'' Mr. Eisbein was back.

"I'm telling about Jacob and my brother Max,'' Grandfather said mildly.

"Why bother?''

"Paul should know why some members of his family consider his great-uncle a renegade.''

"That bunch! What do you expect?'' Mr. Eisbein answered indignantly. "But we're getting away from the subject,'' he added. "You should tell him about the newsstand. I knew the man who owned it before Jacob, a nervous individual; he always wanted something better. He had pinned his hopes on this newsstand on Broadway, in the theatre district. He was disappointed not to be rich already. Jacob stopped to talk to him one evening just after he returned to New York. The occupation appealed to him: it was a simple, useful one. Everyone read newspapers, and in this country, especially in New York, you could buy any kind you wanted. *That* appealed to him too. He bought out the former owner, who went to Miami to seek his fortune; he dropped out of sight. *I'll* tell Paul about Jacob and the newsstand,'' Mr. Eisbein said. "I'll tell him what happened there.''

4

It was early December (Mr. Eisbein said), about a year after Jacob had bought the newsstand, midafternoon of a clear, cold day. The noon rush was over, and at that moment no one wanted to buy a paper; which was just as well, because half the stand's window was blocked by the stout form, round head, and high bowler-shaped helmet of Sergeant O'Toole, the mounted policeman. The rest of the window was occupied by the head of the sergeant's great black horse, Fergus, who had thrust his nose into the newsstand to take a lump of sugar that Jacob had offered him from the copper bowl beside his samovar.

Yes, a real Russian samovar, a high brass one with enameled handles, heated by a small charcoal flame. A few glasses hung beside it for any guests; Sergeant O'Toole had just refused a second glass of tea.

With agile lips, Fergus took the lump of sugar from Jacob's hand. Sergeant O'Toole frowned and massaged his thick red mustache. The sergeant often confided in Jacob when the events he witnessed troubled his simple, upright spirit. This time he had no degradation or cruelty to report, but still, something disturbing. "They broke into Macy's again last night," he whispered.

"And did they take anything this time?" Jacob asked him.

For the past few days the puzzled sergeant had been telling him of signs of illegal entry into the great new store recently erected on Broadway eight blocks downtown from his newsstand. Some person or persons had certainly entered the store: a chair had been moved, draperies in an office had been drawn aside and not closed again, cigar ashes lay in an expensive Meissen dish. Somehow, the new burglar alarms had remained silent. There were no signs that any locks had been tampered with, and nothing had been taken. After the second entry, the store owners, fearing that some extensive robbery was being planned, had installed absolutely burglar-proof locks on the doors and placed three extra watchmen on duty. But this did not prevent a third entry, again with nothing missing. A bottle of Scotch whisky had been opened, it was true, and someone had made a picnic of Norwegian sardines and bottled artichoke hearts. The police could not understand how any criminals who could so easily enter the store did not take more care to conceal signs of their visit. The fourth entry, last night, had been different.

"They did indeed take something," Sergeant O'Toole said. "They took the window dummies."

"The window dummies!" Jacob exclaimed. "You don't mean the mannequins?"

"That's what I do mean, however you call them," the sergeant replied. Jacob stared at him, open-mouthed.

As part of their fall sales program, Macy's had imported some mannequins from England. The three appeared in one window: beautiful young people in formal clothes, a man and woman dancing together while a second taller, dreamy man with a champagne glass in his hand stood a little apart, staring into the street as if he expected a girl of his own to appear.

At that time, such displays were uncommon; whenever Jacob passed the window, he would notice the early-morning people, or the late-night ones, stopping to stare in. He always stopped too. In fact, he now realized, he often walked out of his way to pass the window. He always looked forward to seeing the mannequins and left them with regret. Now Sergeant O'Toole's words dismayed him: light was gone from a bright image in his mind.

The sergeant didn't notice how sad Jacob's face had become. "And not only the dummies," he said in an official voice. "There's a great list of missing items." He drew out a thick notebook. "Six suits of men's evening clothes, four of them with tails. Three top hats. Canes, one with a silver head, two of the knobby kind. Four ladies' ballroom dresses in pink, green, and two shades of gray. A number of more ordinary dresses and some unmentionable articles. Two shelves of costume jewelry: too many individual items to mention, though I have them all here." He flipped over a page. "Musical instruments: three flutes, two harmonicas, a German violin with bow and case. A portable pipe organ, small but heavy all the same — how did they hide it? A croquet set; a hammock; several lawn ornaments; and the list's not done yet!"

Sergeant O'Toole folded his notebook. "The detectives think the thieves may plan to open a shop themselves, and use the same window dummies for decorations. If they do, we'll catch them for sure!" He looked at his great pocket watch. "I must be on my rounds," he added. "I'm on day duty now." He swung himself onto Fergus's back — a light and nimble motion for so big a man — and rode off, leaving Jacob sitting between a pile of the *Times* and a pile of the *Tribune*. He thought sadly about the mannequins, hoping that the thieves would not harm them, before he raised his eyes to watch the world go by.

If you had looked past Jacob to the back of his stand, you might have found almost any paper at all, hanging on rows of string: Hungarian papers, Italian, Yiddish, Spanish, even Japanese ones.

("Did he have comics?" Paul asked. "Why not?" said Mr. Eisbein. "He even had a few naughty magazines, for those people who needed such things but were too shy to go to the regular outlets." Paul giggled. "Watch it, Abe," Grandfather said.)

But now Jacob was looking out at the street (Mr. Eisbein said), and at that time he had something to look at, too! His stand was on Broadway itself, just north of the Times Building, which had been built only a few years before. These days he'd see nothing but cabs and trucks and diesel exhaust fumes. But

31

then he would have looked out on a noble space in a noble city, a space laid out as if there were all the room in the world. Two wide roads, Broadway and Seventh Avenue, came together gently, crossed, and passed leisurely into the distance between high buildings. And to the north, uptown, there were even empty spaces between some buildings. Can you imagine that? Vacant lots in New York City! That's how long ago it was.

Heavy hoofs clattered on the pavement. Four great brown horses drew a wide charabanc from the suburbs: "Greenwich Tours. See Manhattan Island." Gaping heads appeared in the vehicle's windows. In front of Rector's fashionable restaurant, just beside Jacob's newsstand, a gloomy waiter swept the sidewalk, then shook his broom at the tourists. Pigeons and seagulls fluttered over the street looking for scraps.

From between a double row of high, square taxis drawn up before the Times Building a strange figure approached whom Jacob had seen only in the last few days but who seemed more familiar than that: a squat woman, made yet bulkier by layer on layer of sweaters, a heavy cloth bag in each hand. Jacob had seen her leading a group of old men through the alleys off Broadway, probably to scavenge in the restaurant garbage cans. He shook his head: that people should be forced to such tricks in this great, rich city!

A chattering line of schoolchildren holding on to each other's coats passed along Broadway, looking only at the theatre marquees. At the Criterion Theatre, on the corner of 43rd Street, *The Hoosier Girl* was playing, a romantic comedy set in Indiana. At the New York Theatre on the same block was *The Sands of Guantanamo Bay*, a stirring drama glorifying the war by which the United States had restored justice to Cuba.

(Grandfather, who had been nodding off, suddenly opened his eyes. "I remember that one! The young man was frightened, but he loved a Cuban girl, a white one, of an old Spanish family. That turned him into a hero: he killed a whole battalion of the enemy." Mr. Eisbein drew in his breath impatiently. "Such *narrischkeit*! That means 'foolishness,'" he explained to Paul. "That's how all the plays were then: not a real thought in any of them. People didn't want to be disturbed in their comfort."

But Grandfather said, a little apologetically, "I enjoyed it at the time.")

Everybody enjoyed the theatre at that time. Jacob could always spot the theatregoers: they looked like children on the way to a party. When they bought a paper, their eyes shone, as if the news would have to be good. At such times, Jacob felt he was giving each one of his customers a gift.

Now it grew dark; dim streetlights went on. A cold, dry wind arrived from the north. Jacob turned up the little kerosene heater at his feet. A pleasant smell of wood smoke entered his newsstand as Gonzalo, the silent chestnut vendor, wheeled his little cart past it.

The true business of the district began. Lobby doors opened; theatregoers began to arrive on foot and in iron-railed streetcars. Some watched as the leading lady of *The Hoosier Girl*, in a dark sealskin coat, entered the Criterion Theatre from an open carriage. The crowd before the New York Theatre gazed at the new electric sign above the marquee that advertised *The Sands of Guantanamo Bay*. This was one of the first moving electric signs: a battleship on one side fired a shell, a trajectory of light that caused an answering flash from a cluster of palm trees on the other side of the sign — a playful explosion.

Across the square, a little way down 43rd Street, west of Seventh Avenue, Jacob could see the marquee of the Xanadu, a new theatre especially designed for spectacular musical shows. The present one, *Great Gotham Follies*, presented many pretty girls, young men in top hats, four blackface comedians, and three dancing ostriches. Sergeant O'Toole was infatuated with one of the dancing girls. One night he had guided her to the stage door through a crowd attracted by a false rumor that Sarah Bernhardt would appear. The memory of the slender body, the light, strong hand that held his arm as he cleared a path through the mob, while great Fergus brought up the rear, had swelled and deepened. Since she had touched his uniform he thought it a sacrilege to have it cleaned. As often as possible he stationed himself near the stage door before and after performances, in the hope of seeing her again.

But tonight the sergeant was off duty. Out of sympathy with

33

his friend, Jacob kept an eye out for the dancer. Now, at the entrance to 43rd Street, another figure appeared: a tall, hawk-faced man in a long woollen coat. A beggar. Jacob had recently seen him accosting shoppers in a haughty fashion, but had the odd feeling that he had also seen him many years before. The light on the beggar's sharp face showed he was looking directly at the newsstand; perhaps he would cross the square now. Jacob reached for some change. But the beggar turned aside disdainfully and vanished in the shadows.

Customarily, a group of brighter streetlights near each theatre was turned on an hour before the curtains rose; this helped patrons descending from carriages and discouraged pickpockets. The marquee of the Xanadu Theatre suddenly reflected these lights. Jacob blinked, then noticed three unfamiliar figures. They were street dancers or musicians, one of the groups that performed for queues waiting outside the theatres. One of them, a tall, slender man dressed in formal evening clothes — he must be cold, Jacob thought — was playing a flute, while the other two, a shorter man and a young woman, danced in each other's arms. The sound of the flute, a melancholy and sensuous Arabian melody, reached Jacob's ears through the honking of taxis and the policemen's whistles.

Now the dancing couple separated. The tall man and the short man joined hands and circled together, while the girl beat out the steps on a small drum hanging at her waist. Then she joined the short man again, dancing close to him while the tall man played his flute. This changing of partners was repeated several times. The short man played no instrument, and he never danced alone but always, very stiffly, with one of the others. Finally, the two men stood together and the girl traveled, whirling and curtsying, down the queue, while her audience applauded, tossing coins and even bills on to the head of her drum.

Then the dancers left the Xanadu Theatre and crossed over to the Broadway side of the square, the tall man carrying a large blue canvas bag. They walked in a row, arms about each other, but, oddly enough, the short man, not the girl, was in the

34

middle. He walked in a strange, stiff fashion. Perhaps the poor man was crippled, Jacob thought. If so, he had certainly mastered his condition to dance so well with the others. Jacob looked at the dancers more closely. Their faces seemed familiar, but he was sure he had never spoken to them.

Now they stood before the New York Theatre. Here, their dance was quite different. The short man stood, very straight and still, holding a large American flag on a collapsible staff, taken out of the blue canvas bag. The tall man and the girl began to play and march, one after another; the tall man played a shrill fife for the girl, while she beat her drum for him. They marched back and forth, saluting the flag each time they passed it. At first their steps were those of shambling yokels, recruits at the beginning of training. Then their march became tighter, more disciplined, fiercer. They strutted, their chins lifted toward the marquee, as if saluting *The Sands of Guantanamo Bay* or the sign that showed a shell crashing into a defenseless shore. They sneered at those watching, daring them to interfere. Finally, they stood on either side of the short man — whose flagstaff, Jacob now saw, was fastened to his back — and threw his arms over their shoulders. Then, three in line, fife, flag, and drum, they marched up and down the sidewalk. The crowd applauded enthusiastically. The girl took a top hat from the blue canvas bag and moved among them. Coins flashed in the air; she moved so quickly and cleverly that she caught them all; not one escaped.

But Jacob, watching the short dancer, suddenly realized that he had not really been marching at all: the others had carried him along, his legs dangling. Occasionally this gave an impression of walking, but this dancer could not walk by himself. He was not alive; he never had been. He was, in fact, one of the mannequins from Macy's window, the short one who had been dancing with the girl! The other two dancers must have stolen him for their act.

Well, thought Jacob, that was a daring thing to do! And to parade him right here in the square, where anyone might recognize him! The clothes they were wearing, the flute, the fife, the drum, the flag, must all be stolen too. Jacob looked round anxiously for Sergeant O'Toole, then remembered he was off duty. He looked even more anxiously for Constable Tertis, known as the Tiger of Times Square. The constable would certainly have no mercy on theft, especially on such imaginative theft. He had no use for any kind of wrongdoer. His stated ambition was to "clear all the trash off the square." Now he was probably scouring the back alleys for any beggars and derelicts.

At that moment the three dancers walked toward Jacob's newsstand. He could look more closely at the mannequin. He had known its limbs were movable, of course, since its position had changed each week in the store window. But the others must have loosened them further, so that with some help the mannequin could seem to walk and throw its arms about. These thieves were clever workmen! As they passed before his newsstand, the girl looked at him for an instant, then turned her head away. Jacob's heart knocked. For a foolish moment he had thought he recognized that look! The dancers proceeded past the Times Building and disappeared round the corner of 41st Street.

Jacob shook his head. This was something new, even for Broadway! He turned to Gonzalo, the chestnut vendor, who was poking up his fire so that sparks illumined his dark face, and opened his mouth, then closed it again. Though he often discussed the day's events with Gonzalo, this was the time to be silent. Why should *he* call attention to the stolen mannequin? He only hoped the dancers would not be discovered too soon: he wanted to see them again.

And the next evening, there they were. As soon as the brighter lights were turned on, the trio appeared, walking together up Broadway. They circled once round Jacob's newsstand, not twenty feet away. He was serving a line of customers and couldn't really look at them. But what Jacob noticed in one quick glance was that the short mannequin, who had been placed on the outer side of the tall man, was moving much more easily; somehow, they had made its limbs more flexible, so that it almost looked alive. When the last customer had bought his paper and Jacob could really look at the dancers, they were standing by the queue at the Criterion Theatre for *The Hoosier Girl*.

This play told the story of a simple and beautiful young lady on a farm in Indiana: one of those farms with five hundred acres, cows, pigs, shining red cultivators, and enough capital invested to buy a residential block of a small upstate city. The young lady had three suitors. One was a student from the big city, too smart for his own good, impractical, with radical tendencies. Then there was a wealthy man with apartments in New York and London; and a country boy from a neighboring farm, a strong, simple, honest, stupid fellow who had loved the girl all his life. In the end, of course, the girl chose the country boy. The audience loved it.

Now Jacob saw that the dancers were dancing out their own version of the play. The girl wore a dress of brown checked gingham with puffy sleeves and a wide straw sunbonnet. With one hand she applied a bouquet of dried flowers to her nose.

Her first suitor, the student, danced round her playing a Bach gavotte on his flute. He was dressed in a closely buttoned black suit and a flat cap. He gave the girl a book, an interesting rock, an original poem, and a silhouette of the goddess Minerva. She accepted each gift politely and laid it at her feet, yawning.

While this was going on, the mannequin remained standing upright, propped on an upturned pitchfork, one of whose tines passed under the shoulder strap of his overalls. He wore a red bandanna with white polka dots, and a frayed straw hat through which his hair protruded. Jacob stared at him, then at the student, who had just presented the girl with a small stuffed owl.

Then Jacob started to tremble; blood buzzed in his ears. His knees grew so limp that he had to grasp the counter. Very carefully, he lowered the shutter at the front of his newsstand and left the stand, locking the door behind him. He walked slowly toward the dancers, not looking at them again until he was close enough to learn if what he thought he had seen was true.

Yes, it was so: again there were two living dancers and one

mannequin. But this time the mannequin was not the short young man but the tall one! The short young man, very much alive, was changing his clothes, while the young woman, who now had the flute, played "Believe Me, If All Those Endearing Young Charms." He unbuttoned his student jacket, revealing a gleaming dress shirt beneath, and quickly drew a black tailcoat, a top hat, and a cane with a silver handle from the blue canvas bag. Now he was the wealthy suitor. He danced round the girl, then scornfully round the tall, rustic young man, who didn't seem to notice. He couldn't: the tall young man was not alive, he was a mannequin. The overalls, the pitchfork, the hay in his hair could not disguise the fact that this was the tall manne-quin Jacob had seen in Macy's window. And the living young man, who now offered the girl a rich coral necklace, which she dangled from the end of her flute, resembled nothing so much as the short mannequin he had seen in the store window — if that mannequin could come to life and dance in the street.

This could not be! Jacob turned away and entered his newsstand. It was some minutes before he was able to reopen the shutters. Even then, he did not immediately look at the dancers.

There must be some natural, rational explanation, Jacob told himself. After all, this was America. Here, mannequins from department store windows could not come to life. He kept his eyes on the pile of newspapers before him, on a hopeful item about rising prices on the stock market. Then the explanation occurred to him: the dancers were using not only one but two of the stolen mannequins. Therefore, there must be two living young men, each of whom resembled a mannequin closely. Very closely indeed, more so than he would have thought possible. This would account for what he had seen.

But why would they do this, why take such chances? The dancers were skillful indeed. In the regular theatres they would have been stars. And yet they danced here for a few pennies, hardly enough to pay for their meals, poor things! Where could they live, store their props, hide their mannequins so that the police couldn't find them?

And now the dancers were walking toward him again, the short man and the girl supporting between them the tall mannequin, who walked with a shambling gait, still in his rustic dress, with the pitchfork slung over his shoulder and fastened to his overall strap. As the three drew near the newsstand, another curious thing happened.

There was a meager, shriveled beggar of the district, bald except for a flamboyant fringe of white hair, who called himself Sir Stefan. He usually stationed himself by one of the gaslit globes on tall poles that stood before Rector's restaurant. Now he came out of an alleyway. He must have been begging for food at one of the restaurant kitchens, and this time to some purpose: in one hand he bore a cracked dish on which most of a full portion of Chicken Kiev still smoked. In his other hand was a bottle of Beaujolais, half full. With a comfortable step, Sir Stefan walked toward his lamppost. But before he could reach it the girl dancer left the other dancer and the mannequin together and walked toward him. The beggar stopped, and by instinct his hand went out; then he realized it was already full. Something, perhaps the girl's grave beauty, made him hold out the bottle.

"A glass of wine, miss?" he asked.

The girl smiled, touched her finger to her lips, and said the word "marigold."

"What?" Sir Stefan exclaimed.

The girl shook her head. She walked to one side of the beggar and repeated "marigold." She said the word again at his back, and at his other side, then rejoined her companions.

Sir Stefan, open-mouthed, watched them walk away. Then, shaking his head, he sat down beside his lamppost. He spread a newspaper over his knees, took a chipped long-stemmed glass from an inner pocket, filled it, and sniffed the bouquet. Before drinking, he looked into the front window of Rector's restaurant. A family birthday party was in progress. The daughter, about fourteen, a slim, pale-haired girl with blue eyes ablaze in the restaurant's light, sat at the head of the table. Her parents and brothers watched her; she looked at the sparkling cake a waiter had just set before her. Sir Stefan raised his glass, waiting till she cut the cake before he turned to his own plate.

But a shadow fell over him; two high black shoes, two strong blue legs cut off his light. "So," said Constable Tertis, "enjoying our little repast, are we?"

The constable drew back his foot and kicked expertly. Only the top of the wineglass flew away. "What a pity!" said the constable. "But it wouldn't be good manners to drink it straight from the bottle." He swung his nightstick; the bottle shattered in Sir Stefan's hands. "Why, you old bum!" The constable kicked the plate away. "You aren't fit to eat on the same sidewalk as decent folk!" He stamped on the chicken breast. "Now you clean all that up!" He reached for the beggar's shoulders, but Sir Stefan scuttled away, a short, white streak, out of sight down the alley. The constable started to follow, then stopped.

"He's back where he belongs," Constable Tertis announced with satisfaction. "I wouldn't lower myself by chasing him there." He looked at the two dancers and the mannequin, who had stopped half a block away. "Move on, move on!" he said. The girl looked angrily at him; her short companion touched her arm. Much to Jacob's relief, the three dancers did move on.

But this incident remained in his mind, too. Could the word "marigold" have been intended as a charm, a spell by which the dancing girl had wished to bring the beggar luck? "In the old country, such words often didn't work either," Jacob thought sadly. "They must have used the wrong word this time."

5

❧

Jacob knew he would see the dancers again; it was only a question of time. But one day passed, then another, in which the great bustling square remained empty of them and, to him, seemed empty indeed.

Early on the afternoon of the third day, the familiar walls of the newsstand began to close round him like those of a prison. The newspapers hanging on their strings stirred and rustled menacingly. He heard their pages humming as if each paper were speaking in its own language. "Well, I'm getting too dull here," he said to himself. "I have strange fancies; I'd better take a walk to clear my head."

This was a Wednesday afternoon, normally a busy time with all the matinees. Indeed, as he locked his newsstand door, a line of ladies in light-green coats, each of whom wore a diagonal white band with "Rye Garden Club" written in darker green letters, started to veer toward his stand. But when he left the door closed—with an apologetic shake of his head—the line of ladies straightened and continued amicably south on Broadway, toward the group of theatres known as the Rialto district. In a moment Jacob followed them.

Lines were forming before all the theatres. The garden ladies, giggling gently, joined a queue by the box office of the Broadway Theatre on 41st Street to see *His Father's Wife*, a daring new drama. Jacob glanced at the marquee but continued down Broadway.

By the Empire Theatre on the next block, where *Sag Harbor* was playing, a short, black, frizzy-haired organ-grinder in red overalls held a clever black monkey on a long chain. The monkey, who also wore red overalls, first danced and capered for the audience, which watched listlessly. Then the monkey held the chain, and the organ-grinder, still winding the handle, danced in turn. Those waiting in line guffawed, slapped each other on the back, and pointed out that they could see no difference between the black man and his monkey; that they had always suspected there *was* no difference. They showered coins into the monkey's cup and at the organ-grinder's head and feet. The grinder retrieved the coins with comic gestures; the monkey brought him the cup and emptied it into his over-all pocket. The black man scratched the monkey's head, and they looked at each other sadly and wisely.

Jacob walked on. All the lines were entering the theatres now, but as Jacob approached the Savoy Theatre on 34th Street, where *Magnolia Blossoms*, a drama of the Old South, had already begun, he saw that a performance was still going on outside. It was being watched by a hot-chestnut vendor, a cab driver in an idle hansom, two small boys with open mouths, a rabbinical student with red beard and black hat, a dumpy woman behind a baby carriage packed with dirty linen, and three sandwich-board men.

Two sickly maples stood on the sidewalk before the theatre. Between them a hammock was slung in which, a wide straw hat shading her face, reclined the girl dancer of Jacob's trio. The two male dancers, banjos in hand, were perched on light folding stools on either side of the hammock. They wore white trousers and white jackets with broad stripes, the tall man's stripes red, the short man's blue. On their heads were flat straw hats with bands of colors matching their jacket stripes. They wore white shoes too, which were very visible at that moment, since they were swinging the hammock to and fro with their feet. As the hammock rose, Jacob saw that a green wooden elf two feet high, a summer lawn figure, stood on the pavement beneath it.

Jacob drew nearer. The men's cheekbones were smudged with black, their lips thickened with red. The tall man sang "Old Black Joe" in a rich, sentimental voice, and in the accents of a blackface comedian. He accompanied himself with solemn chords while the short man played Gounod's "Ave Maria," which, if you didn't know, goes remarkably well with "Old Black Joe."

The audience applauded, the singers bowed and pushed the hammock back and forth rapidly, so that the girl in it seemed to be bowing too. But she couldn't bow. Jacob, who now stood at the foot of the hammock, saw that it was not a living girl but the third mannequin from Macy's window. The two men stopped the hammock at the apex of its backward swing to display its contents better. Jacob looked at the mannequin's face. Yes, it was the same: the same face he had seen in Macy's window, the same as that of the living girl three evenings before. He stared at the face as if it were still alive, as if he had always known it.

The silent face dazzled his eyes. He lowered them to the statue of the elf near his feet, and saw that a red price tag from Macy's was still looped around the crown of its pointed hat. He looked quickly to see if anyone else in the small audience had noticed. No, they were still watching the performers. Jacob stepped forward, slipped the red tag off the elf's hat, and put it in his pocket.

The short man stopped his tune with a harsh chord. "Look dere, what dat Jacob is doing for us! He is shielding us from de police!"

Jacob jerked up his head. It didn't seem odd that the dancer knew his name — many people did. And street musicians, he knew, often teased the audience. But the short man's voice had been that of a girl. Despite the fake Negro accent, it sounded just like the voice that had said "marigold" three evenings ago.

The tall dancer said, "Hush, Mr. Bones, you is not being discreet."

"Don't you call me Mr. Bones, Mr. Interlocutor," the short man replied. "Whatever I is, I is not bones!"

(They were using, Mr. Eisbein explained, the usual formula from minstrel and vaudeville shows: Mr. Bones is the comic and Mr. Interlocutor the one who asks questions, the "straight man.")

"You is embarrassing the man," the tall man said more kindly.

"Jacob wouldn't be embarrassed by a good deed, Mr. Interlocutor." The short man set the hammock swinging again. He began to strum the tune of "Swanee River," then rested the head of his banjo on the ground. "For this I need the music," he complained. "How can I look at the music and swing our friend here?"

"Maybe Jacob can swing her, Mr. Bones," the tall man suggested.

"Yes indeed," the short man said. The two dancers stood and bowed to Jacob; the short dancer twitched the hammock so that the mannequin also seemed to bow. Feeling very foolish, but not knowing how to refuse, Jacob began to swing the hammock to and fro.

And this wasn't all: in a moment the tall man took up a music stand that leaned against the tree, set a large edition of the songs of Stephen Collins Foster on it, and handed the stand to Jacob. He found himself holding the music stand with one hand while he swung the hammock with the other. It was a ridiculous position, but the dancers had so readily made him part of their act that he did not feel able to walk away.

The dancers gathered behind the stand, heads touching, and began "Swanee River." But after singing:

> "All up and down the whole creation
> Sadly I roam,
> Still longing for the old plantation
> And for the old folks at home,"

the short dancer winked at Jacob, played two dissonant chords, then, without accompaniment, sang:

"By asteroid and constellation
I randomly roam,
Searching the niches of a flawed creation
For an acceptable home."

Most of the audience looked puzzled, but the three sandwich-board men applauded happily and clacked their boards against each other.

The tall dancer let his banjo dangle and, very theatrically, put his hand to his forehead. "Lawdy, Mr. Bones, you is taking liberties wid de text!"

"We is street musicians, Mr. Interlocutor. Improvisation falls within our terms of reference."

"Mr. Bones," the tall man said severely. "You is producing obscure verse again. Your public will not understand you."

"Jacob will understand me," the short man said. Both the dancers looked at Jacob.

"He does not understand you now, Mr. Bones," the tall man said.

"He will," the short man said gently. "He will in time."

Both dancers looked at Jacob; their eyes were cool and speculating. He looked away and saw that the audience was restless; some were leaving. He had better leave too, he thought. This part of the act had gone on quite long enough. He carefully placed the music at the foot of the mannequin in the hammock, bowed to the dancers, and walked away.

But when he was halfway down the block the two men began another song, no longer in blackface accent. The words followed him down the street:

"Do you remember
The bridge on the river,
The rock in the horsepond,
The roofs thatched with straw?
The storks on the chimneys,
The stars in the woodsmoke,
The firs and the steeples,
The geese by the door?"

Jacob would have continued walking, perhaps faster than before, but he had to pull himself up short to avoid running into the hawk-faced beggar who stood, smiling, directly in his path. Still dazed by the words of the song, Jacob pulled a coin from his pocket. But the beggar shook his head. "I can't accept that." His accent showed that, as Jacob had suspected, he too was an immigrant.

"No offense," Jacob mumbled. "But aren't you a beggar?"

"Of course I'm a beggar, but I'm not begging now. At this moment I'm listening to a song from the old country, just as you are." Now the beggar moved aside to let Jacob pass, but added as he walked by, "You should stop running away from it."

Jacob returned, musing, to his newsstand. It was a relief to do such a simple thing as accept a coin and sell a newspaper. But the words of the dancers and the hawk-faced beggar buzzed round in his mind like flies that never settle down. He dealt with whoever came to him, took a letter for someone's step-uncle, told a stranger where he might find a clean, cheap hotel; all these actions as if in a dream. The faces that passed before him, his newspapers, his own hands making change, the coins he touched, all seemed gray and shadowy. Lights came on on Broadway: the dim streetlights, then the brighter lights of the theatres. Lines formed before the theatres and vanished inside. Gonzalo pushed his iron-wheeled chestnut cart into place without a rattle. Jacob felt it was growing colder. He turned up his little kerosene heater, pulled his shawl round his shoulders, and waited.

"What's the matter?" Grandfather asked. Paul had snuggled up into his coat. "Are you cold?"

Paul shook his head; though a cloud hid the sun for a moment, the air was still warm. A sunbeam broke through the cloud, struck the roof of the bandstand across the river, and glinted in his eyes. Ever since the three singers in the bandstand had started to tell a story, and then stopped, they had been singing country songs whose tunes were familiar, though he could not make out the words. Now they were not singing, but the notes of their guitars were piercing: sharp twangs in the clear air. Paul moved closer to Grandfather. "Jacob better watch out," he said.

"You think he should watch out, eh?" Mr. Eisbein asked. "That's what any sensible person might think. But Jacob wasn't sensible then. He wasn't afraid of the dancers; he wanted them to come again. He knew they would come."

They came that evening (Mr. Eisbein said), an hour before the plays ended. They came walking up Broadway, up the Rialto. But not as he had seen them that afternoon: no, there was the tall man and the girl, dressed in evening clothes, with the short mannequin between them, also in evening clothes, the same clothes that the three mannequins had worn in Macy's window. They leaned the mannequin against the counter, between them. "Good evening," said the girl, and the tall man said "Good evening" too.

Jacob smiled at the tall man to show he bore no ill feeling for his jokes that afternoon. "Where is your friend?" he asked. "The two of you had a good time with me today."

The tall man also smiled, apologetically. "Asking you to help us was a way of making your acquaintance," he said gently. "We were told to make your acquaintance."

The girl said, "We were told that at this place we would find a small man looking out at the world, like a chipmunk on a rock."

Jacob stared at her. Her voice was certainly that of the shorter dancer that very afternoon. "Who told you?" he whispered.

"We were told. And here you are. We heard that Jacob has newspapers from all over the world."

"How did you know that?"

"Everyone knows that," the girl said.

"I suppose I have a local reputation," said Jacob modestly. "And a newspaper dealer, especially in New York, must have a wide selection."

"Your reputation is much more than local," said the girl.

47

"It is," the tall man affirmed. "We were amazed to learn what a reputation you had," he added in an eager voice. "Amazed, and proud too."

Before Jacob could ask about his "reputation" or their interest in it, the girl added, "But they wonder about you."

"Who wonders?" Jacob asked.

"They do, there."

The tall man added quickly, "They ask, for example, if you are making full use of your talents?"

"Oh, I have no great talents," Jacob said humbly. "I sell newspapers that people need."

The girl nodded. "Even that takes foresight."

"They say," put in the tall man, "that you pass on messages; that you give good advice without prying or being officious; that you sometimes offer small loans, a glass of tea on cold nights, a kind face in this hard city."

" 'They' are too kind, whoever they are," Jacob replied modestly.

"Not so kind as you think," the girl said sharply. "They also ask, is it enough that such a person should only observe, only watch the world go by, only be kind to those who pass his newsstand, however kind he is then? They say, such a man should have a family of his own. Why have you no family, Jacob?"

This seemed very familiar talk from a stranger, but somehow Jacob didn't resent it. He wasn't even angry when she added, "Perhaps you have a cold heart?"

"Not at all!" Jacob answered. "But you know, I found no one I wanted to marry. At least, not in this country."

"A young man like you!" The girl shook her head, as if in disbelief. "Are there no beautiful girls here?"

"Many," Jacob said, though he wasn't sure if he really thought so. Then fairness compelled him to add, "Beautiful, kind, intelligent. But something was always missing."

The girl's mischievous eyes gleamed at him. "Oh, Jacob, Jacob, you have been spoiled!"

The tall man cleared his throat. The girl looked up at him

and winked, but was silent. Jacob too was glad to change the subject. "You should be careful," he whispered, "carrying this mannequin around." He pointed to the short mannequin, not quite touching it. "The police may become suspicious."

"Oh, the police," the girl said lightly. Jacob thought she was dismissing them too easily, but he admired her assurance.

"Where is the third member of your group?" he asked.

"The third one?" The tall man touched the mannequin on its shoulder. "Here it is."

"I meant the third living one," said Jacob. The two living dancers stared at him. "You see," he explained, "I have it figured out. There are three of you, one for each mannequin. In each of your acts that I saw, one of you was absent."

"So that's how we do it, is it, Jacob?" the girl asked.

"It must be. That is the only rational explanation."

"Yes, the only rational explanation," the girl replied. "You are still so fond of explanations, aren't you? Some day you'll learn the true explanation, which is less rational. Suppose I tell you that there are only two of us?"

"That would be impossible."

"But I do tell you. If it is not so, then I am lying."

Jacob said, gently, "People do lie."

"They do indeed. *Here* they always lie; *there*, they can't. *I* am not lying to you. It is forbidden."

Jacob waited for the girl to explain who forbade lying, and where, but she looked round the newsstand. "How many papers you have here!"

"I try to keep a good stock." Jacob was relieved that the conversation was returning to everyday subjects; relieved, but also disappointed.

"I see that," the girl said. "*The Times* of London, *Le Figaro*, papers from Singapore, Athens, Mexico City. Have you any papers, by chance, from the town of Niekapowisko?"

That was the name of Jacob's native village! "There was no paper there," he stammered. "It was too small."

"I know," the girl said. "Small, obscure, dull. Still, things happened there too. Perhaps you have the *Trybuna* of Lublin?"

"No, but I might get it for you. I had friends once," Jacob reminisced, "who always read the *Trybuna*."

"Did they? What parts did they like best?"

"Oh, the theatrical section; they read nothing else."

"Yes," the tall man said suddenly, "the stage in Lublin, in Warsaw."

"In London, Madrid, New York!" said the girl.

Jacob shook his head sadly. "The New York stage. My friends thought some day they would appear in the New York theatres."

"Yes, that always seemed the best of all to us," the tall man said. "We thought, in a wonderful new land anything would be possible."

"Wouldn't it just!" the girl said ironically. She added, "And so we came to the heart of the theatrical world, to New York itself. We always thought that some day we would conquer the New York theatre."

"And here you are," Jacob said encouragingly. "Outside the theatres for the moment; soon you'll be inside."

"We think not," the tall man said. "Mr. Spangler said we should play outside theatres."

"Mr. Spangler? Is he your agent?"

"You might call him that."

"Such an agent!" the girl remarked.

The tall man said, "You may have noticed, we only play outside theatres. We comment on the plays inside."

"I saw that. But with your talents, you should be on the stage itself."

"No, that is impossible."

"It is forbidden," the girl added. "But, after all, the theatre is all make-believe. Now we pretend we might change events in the world outside."

Jacob remembered the little scene with Sir Stefan, the beggar. "For example, you might say the right word at the right time?" The two dancers nodded. "My friends," Jacob said, "the ones who were so fond of the theatre, they tried to find the right word too. It was a game they played."

"Was it only a game?" the girl asked.

"Each word was supposed to be magic," Jacob explained. "It could only be used on one occasion. In the right situation, the correct word could cause a good result; say, good luck for someone."

"The right word might have saved the beggar from the policeman the other night?" the girl suggested.

"You said 'marigold' then; but that didn't work."

"No. The right word was 'trillium.' That's a flower in the northern forest. If I had said 'trillium,' the policeman would never have come; the poor beggar would have eaten in peace."

"Then why didn't you say it?"

The girl did not answer immediately. "I found it hard not to," she said at last.

The tall man added, as if to excuse her behavior: "Mr. Spangler suggested this to us. He said, 'If you use the right word, Jacob won't understand, because nothing will happen. He might appreciate your gesture of goodwill toward the beggar, no more than that. But if you use the wrong word, so that the cruel policeman comes, Jacob will remember. He will remember other words that didn't work, the words "mandrake" and "asafetida," that failed, long ago, to keep two young men out of the army.'"

The two dancers stepped back and looked at Jacob. "If the words had succeeded, we could all have come here together, Jacob," the girl said softly.

Jacob looked into her eyes, then into the eyes of the tall man, then into her eyes again, as if he had never left them. His next words made no sense at all. "You did come to New York, Simon. You did come, Esther," he said.

The tall man smiled. The girl touched Jacob's cheek. "We did come, Jacob," she said. "Sometimes you are not so stupid, after all."

Jacob shook his head quickly. "But this can't be!" He looked desperately at the mannequin. "Who is the third one? The one I saw this afternoon?"

51

"Now you are stupid again, Jacob," the girl said. "Always looking for a rational explanation. Watch the third one."

Jacob looked. Indeed, it was impossible not to obey. And as he watched, in an instant the fixed eyes of the mannequin blinked; they took on life; the mannequin stood upright and spoke. "It was I," said the girl's voice. "But now look at what I was." Jacob saw that where the living girl had been was now the mannequin of the girl, whom the tall man supported by the arm. "Keep watching her," the girl's voice said. The girl mannequin blinked and stood upright; the mannequin of the short man again slumped against the counter.

"I can do that too, Jacob," said the tall man. The short mannequin became alive again and said, with a deep voice, "I am here." The girl held the tall mannequin upright. Then, no longer a mannequin, it shook its head. "And now I am back."

Jacob shook his head. "Enough tricks! I think I believe you now!" He looked at the three of them, the two living ones and the mannequin. "Why," he demanded at last, "did you take the third mannequin from the window if there are only two of you?"

The two dancers fell silent. Finally the girl said, dryly, "Mr. Spangler told us to take the third one. He wouldn't explain why."

The man added in a kinder voice, "He said it would be a pity to leave it alone."

"I know what he *said*." The girl turned to Jacob. "The theatres are closed now. We must go."

"But you'll come back?" Jacob asked anxiously.

"Oh yes, we'll come back, Jacob," the tall man said.

"We'll come back," said the girl softly.

"You must," said Jacob. "You see, I've been so lonely."

"We have, too, Jacob," the girl said.

6

Paul said, "I know why they took all three dummies."

Mr. Eisbein, looking dazed, turned slowly toward him, but before he could ask Paul to explain, Grandfather said, "Take it easy, Abe."

Mr. Eisbein blinked. His pupils were small, his eyes distant, as if he had been staring into the sun. Paul saw that his forehead was so flushed that the brown and blue spots hardly showed; a small blood vessel on his temple beat busily. Gradually Mr. Eisbein's eyes focused on Grandfather. "Do you think I should? Am I talking too much?"

"You could be quiet for a bit," Grandfather said. "It wouldn't hurt."

Mr. Eisbein nodded. He pressed his shoulders against the bench, closed his eyes, and began to breathe slowly and regularly, as Paul had seen him do before when he got too excited.

Paul heard a new sound, or rather a new texture of sound. The guitars across the river were silent. Mr. Eisbein seemed to be listening closely to the silence, and Grandfather too. The air hummed around them, probably feedback from the P.A. system, Paul thought. But when the voice of the girl singer crossed the river, it seemed clear and direct, without any amplification. The girl began:

"Trains at dawn that say hello,
Midnight trains that hum goodbye
Take my love to other lands
Through the spaces of the sky."

The guitars twanged a country chorus. Then the two men
sang:

"I am waiting at the station
With the milk cans and the sawdust
Till a shabby blue conductor
Beckons from a passing window."

The girl sang:

"There's a message from your lover:
He can't stop by here today.
If you go to other lands,
You may meet him in the station,
You may meet him on the ferry,
You may meet him at the crossroads,
You may meet him on the way."

Across the river, people continued to flow round the bandstand as if they had not heard the song. On the near bank, the
row of frogs stirred, like a moving wave of green. Mr. Eisbein
shook himself. "Yes, that's how it was," he said quietly. "As if
they were meeting at some little railway station, between nowhere and nowhere."

Now Grandfather cleared his throat. "That last conversation,
between Jacob and his friends. Who could have heard that?"

"What?" Mr. Eisbein asked.

"That was a very private conversation. Jacob might have
told other people about the rest, about his feelings."

"He did," Mr. Eisbein said.

"But not that conversation. Jacob would have kept it to
himself; he would have treasured it."

"That's right," Mr. Eisbein nodded gravely. "But maybe
Jacob wasn't *able* to keep the conversation to himself. I remember now. It all came out in Tannenbaum's dream."

"Which Tannenbaum?" Grandfather asked.

"The religious-goods salesman."

"I didn't know him."

"Why should you?" Mr. Eisbein asked. "But I knew him well. He was a tiny man with well-cut shoes, beautifully polished, and a great case of silver- and gold-plated crucifixes that he always clutched tight under his arm. He kept late hours, and sometimes he'd wait for his streetcar by the newsstand when it was closed and Times Square was almost empty. He'd sleep standing up at the streetcar stop. Passersby saw him and some even spoke to him, but only the car's bell woke him.

"At the time I'm talking about, just before Christmas when his business was especially good, he waited for his streetcar three nights in a row. And each night he had this dream: he'd see Jacob in his newsstand and the two dancers and the mannequin, and hear every word they said. It was all so clear, he was sure he was really seeing them, but when he opened his eyes there was only the empty street and the empty newsstand. The words made very little sense to him, out of context, but he remembered them. It seems they were important enough, somewhere, to get themselves repeated."

Mr. Eisbein rubbed his chin and shook his head. "There were other conversations that Tannenbaum heard, too. He didn't remember all the words, but he was more impressed with the sound of the voices than the words themselves. It was the voices of men, he said, five or six of them, and they seemed to be speaking from very far away. There was a hollow sound around their voices, what would be called a 'celestial' sound in the movies now. But what they said reminded him more of the conversation of a bunch of petty gamblers in a bookie's office.

"Tannenbaum said they were talking about a Central Betting Office somewhere, and about this Mr. Spangler the dancers had just been discussing. They called him 'Stephen Spangler' with a little sneer, as if he were using an alias. It seemed he had made a bet about a certain newsdealer, what he would do, what decision he would reach. And the stakes of the bet weren't money, but stars and comets and galaxies. They were discussing what the odds were, what they should be, what Stephen Spangler's chances were of winning. Tannenbaum couldn't figure out what they were talking about, but that part of his dream made him very uneasy, and he didn't like to talk about it. He seemed glad to put it out of his mind."

Grandfather didn't seem so ready to put it out of his mind. "So, they were placing bets, up there, about what Jacob would do?" he asked.

"So it seemed," Mr. Eisbein replied.

"But what decision were they betting on for Jacob?"

"I think I know," Mr. Eisbein said. "But he wasn't bothered with that decision yet, right after he talked to the dancers. First he had another one to make: if he really believed that his friends had come back. The atmosphere of the afternoon and night had made him believe that the spirits of his friends Simon and Esther were walking around in two of the three mannequins stolen from Macy's window. But next morning the clear light made everything seem different. Jacob had to be convinced all over again."

What you believe at night (Mr. Eisbein continued), when it seems that the voices of those you loved call to you from the city's darkness, this is different from what you will believe by the clear light of morning. Jacob, in his newsstand, watching the everyday world pass before him, felt foolish and gullible. A streetcar clanged and rattled down Broadway. Its iron wheels seemed to say, "We too can strike sparks from nothing."

Sergeant O'Toole, solid and foursquare, patrolled on Fergus's back by the uptown end of the square. Jacob knew that the sergeant was happy: that morning his dancer had smiled at him as she entered the foyer of the Xanadu Theatre. Twice, the sergeant had told Jacob, she had waved at him from a window. Looking at the corner of the theatre now, Jacob saw the dancer's face, round, pretty, anxious, as she waited for Sergeant O'Toole to come in sight again.

No, thought Jacob, there were honest folk like the sergeant,

whose friends were of this world; friends with simple, true feelings even in this place of illusions. But he himself had been taken in. Everything was false here: the theatres were only designed to make the world seem better than it was. That was all the public wanted. The old men back in his village, who had so distrusted the theatre and the other things of this world, had been right.

He didn't know how the dancers had done it, how they had imitated so well the looks and voices of his dead friends. They seemed to know what no one else could have known. But, after all, he had thought these matters were private because they concerned him so. Still, he was not the only one who had come to America from his little village. He would have sworn that Simon and Esther had told no one but him the secret of their play with the prince, the princess, and the magic word; but perhaps only vanity had made him think so. Other people must have heard it, and so the story came to America.

But what purpose could they have in fooling him, what cruel purpose?

And this trick of mannequins who seemed to take on and lose the breath of life: probably there were no mannequins at all, but living people who pretended to be mannequins. Actors could do wonderful things. He couldn't think why they would choose to do this, but it was the only rational explanation. When he saw the dancers again, Jacob decided, he would touch the mannequin, whichever one it was this time. Thus, he would satisfy himself that, however stiff and lifeless it seemed, it was really alive. With impatience and fear he waited for the dancers to come.

They came early enough. Directly across the square from his newsstand, on Seventh Avenue, was a small French restaurant, The Three Knocks. Its front was recessed from those of the neighboring buildings, forming a narrow courtyard from whose pavement a thin brown willow sprouted. Tables stood round the courtyard; most were cluttered with newspapers and debris, but one had been cleared. At it sat the three dancers, or the two dancers and the mannequin, if it was one; again, the short

dancer who sat staring away from the others, looking slack and foolish. All were dressed in stylish light clothing with light topcoats. Also at the table was a stout older man in a dark suit. He wore a heavy, dark overcoat and a derby hat that sat symmetrically on his round head.

The tall dancer — Jacob could not think of him as Simon or of the girl as Esther — waved to Jacob to join them. He shook his head politely. The girl waved at him too; again he refused. The two dancers spoke to the stout man, who turned around and stared at Jacob. He had a moon face, a small trim mustache, and — at that distance — an expression of amiable stupidity. He turned back to the others. In a moment they were walking across the square toward Jacob's newsstand. The two dancers had quickly stacked four chairs on the tabletop; then they carried the table and chairs across the square. No one in the restaurant stopped them.

Left behind, the moon-faced man looked down at the third dancer, or the mannequin, scratched his head under the derby hat, then touched the mannequin's hand and led it toward the newsstand. He didn't seem to support it at all, and Jacob thought, "It *must* be alive."

The two dancers placed the table and chairs on the sidewalk before the newsstand. The stout man, holding the third mannequin — or dancer — by the hand and propping himself on a cane, watched the operation from the street.

"Mr. Spangler likes to be comfortable," the girl told Jacob. "He insisted that we bring the table over."

"You can't talk business just standing around in the street." The stout man settled himself and the mannequin at the table. He had a hoarse, anxious voice, as if he expected someone to challenge every word.

"Are we talking business?" the girl asked. "You said you wanted to *meet* Jacob."

"Meeting people is my business now," the stout man replied innocently. "But I have some other business with him, too."

"I understand you're a theatrical agent," Jacob said stiffly.

"Correct. I have a card somewhere." The stout man searched

among his coats and vest and finally came up with a soiled card which he passed on to Jacob: "Stephen Spangler, Theatrical Agent, Seeks and Places Unusual Talent," with an address on 47th Street. While Jacob read this, the stout man watched a line of people by the streetcar stop. "Maybe you could play something for them?" he suggested to the tall dancer.

"They wouldn't like it, Mr. Spangler," the dancer said respectfully.

"They wouldn't? Why not? They looked bored. Amuse them!"

"They *are* bored," the girl said. "Also tired of waiting. They just want their streetcar to come. They'd resent any kind of distraction."

"Do you think so? You could try. Even a few nickels would help."

"It wouldn't work, Mr. Spangler," the girl said firmly.

Mr. Spangler shook his head, sour, not convinced. At that moment, several customers stopped to buy papers; all took the *Times*. They looked at the table and its occupants and departed.

"Now, those people are not bored or impatient," Mr. Spangler said. "Also, they have coins in their hands. You might play something for them. Yes," he said to Jacob, brightening up, "you could sell the papers just a little slower; put them out of sight, pretend to search for them. A small queue would form, people who would enjoy a bit of music. Everyone has a coin ready for a paper; if one, why not two?"

"Mr. Spangler," the girl interrupted, "you mustn't interfere with Jacob's business."

Mr. Spangler sighed. "I agree, I agree. I also said I wouldn't ask him to store your things in his newsstand between acts; though I still don't see why."

"It would make him accessory to theft, that's why," the girl said.

"True, theft. I'm a thief." Here the stout man giggled. "Well, why not, since those were my instructions? I may have been the first of us who was ever a thief," he said proudly. He smoothed down his mustache and his melancholy brown eyes brightened as he added, "It was so easy." Then he knitted his brows. "But why not do a few extra turns for these lines?" he persisted. "You might collect *something*."

"We have no legal status on the street," the girl said patiently.

"No?" The stout man seemed surprised. "Should we have?"

"We are only tolerated here. They don't mind if we put on our act for the theatre queues; it's traditional, the people like it. But if we began to bother others, to beg, to make nuisances of ourselves, the police would drive us away."

Mr. Spangler nodded gravely, not agreeing or disagreeing. He said, "My landlord was very unpleasant this morning."

"Didn't the money come?" the tall man asked sympathetically.

"Not yet. No word from the Accounting Office. Who knows how long? Time means nothing there! 'A million dollars is as a penny; a million years is as a second.' They can condense gold from air, but who knows when I'll get it? They must be saying, 'Wait a second.' And the forms I had to fill out! I made just a little mistake in the last one and they sent it back. Still, they answered."

"Of course they did," the tall man reassured him. "They won't leave you stranded here."

"And I don't like the decorations," Mr. Spangler said. "The Artefacts and Fabrications Office must have got them from a catalogue: 'One theatrical agent's office.' I could use more lamps; a better chair, my back hurts; even a couch for a refreshing nap." He looked shyly at the girl. "I was thinking of another trip to Macy's."

The girl shook her head firmly. "It was just a thought," Mr. Spangler said quickly. "Someone came to the office today," he added. "The manager of a theatre on 14th Street. He asked for you, for the three of you. He wanted you for a spot in his vaudeville program. He told me a man from Weber and Fields comes to watch all his shows for new talent. I had to refuse. It would have meant a hundred-dollar commission just to sign you on. A hundred dollars!"

"Really? Weber and Fields?" the tall dancer asked eagerly. "Can we do it?"

"I'm sorry, no. I checked again. It's forbidden. The answer came back right away. Imagine," Mr. Spangler said, "a negative answer comes immediately. For operating funds they take forever!"

The figures of Fergus and Sergeant O'Toole towered suddenly above the table. "You'll have to move the furniture back, sir," the sergeant said in a firm but kind voice. "You know it belongs to the restaurant. You're lucky no one's complained yet. I don't want to take official notice, but have it gone when I pass here again." He winked at Jacob and rode on.

Mr. Spangler ran his forefinger round his hat brim, then pointed the finger at the departing horse and rider. Jacob saw a strange thing happen to both of them: the sergeant's coat quivered as if his muscles were filling out beneath it. Fergus trembled and his black figure lost its sharp outline for a moment. Then it was as clear as before, clearer. His step was lighter, more springy. Mr. Spangler remarked to Jacob, "I've just given the man ten good years, and five to his horse.

"You understand," he added, anxious to be accurate, "I said 'good' years; not 'more' years. I can't extend life: that isn't in my terms of reference. I can only improve its quality. But let me show you something really unusual."

Mr. Spangler snapped his fingers, and suddenly a pack of cards appeared in his hand. Jacob supposed he had kept it inside his sleeve, though he was surprised that such a clumsy person could produce the cards so smoothly. Mr. Spangler rose from the table and walked to the newsstand. He spread the cards out on the counter, his thick fingers separating them with difficulty. "Now," he said, "take any three cards and put them back in the pack. But remember them. You have to remember them."

"Oh no, Mr. Spangler!" the girl said. "Not that trick again!"

"I've been practicing," the agent said with dignity. "It should work this time."

Jacob obligingly took the ace of spades, the jack of diamonds, and the two of clubs and put them back in the pack. Mr. Spangler kept his eyes lowered, but the newsdealer was sure he peeked. The agent shuffled the pack twice, sat at the table again, and dealt the cards out in a complicated pattern which he sheltered from the wind between his elbows. He studied the cards. "Queen of diamonds, ten of spades, seven of clubs?" he asked hopefully.

"No," Jacob said. "I'm sorry," he added.

"It should have worked. I don't know why it didn't work." Mr. Spangler did not seem embarrassed. "Now, here's another one." He threw his arm upward, so that his overcoat sleeve covered the table for an instant. When he lowered his arm, Jacob saw that a large top hat rested on the table. "I really made it appear from nowhere," Mr. Spangler explained earnestly. "I was told to make the pass with my arm so that you might think I used sleight of hand. That's a standard magician's illusion, you know."

Suddenly, the brim of the hat lifted and made a half-circle, then the hat tilted to one side, and a large black rabbit and an even larger white chicken that must somehow have fitted into it leaped out onto the table. The chicken flew up and perched on one of the gas globes, fortunately unlighted, before Rector's restaurant. The shrivelled beggar, Sir Stefan, who sat at the foot of the pole that supported the gas globe, looked up suspiciously and drew his hat firmly over his ears. The rabbit shook its ears indignantly, leaped off the table, and lolloped past Sir Stefan's feet.

"Rabbit!" Sir Stefan cried. "I love rabbit!" He scrambled to his feet and scuttled after the rabbit. As they turned the corner of 46th Street, the beggar seemed to be gaining.

The failure of Mr. Spangler's second trick, whatever he had planned, made it easier for Jacob to say what he had to. "I said some foolish things last night," he told the girl.

"You don't have to worry about that, Jacob," she answered kindly. "You saw the truth soon enough."

"I didn't quite mean that. I do admire your skill. How could you ever give such illusions? But I must say it was cruel, too: to make me think you were my friends, or the spirits of my friends, from the old country."

"And what else were we?"

"Clever actors, the cleverest I ever heard of. You could even make yourselves seem to be dry, stiff mannequins." Jacob looked at the third one, the short dancer or mannequin, slumped in its chair, as if he expected it to rise on these words.

The girl walked to the short figure, twisted its arm, and pulled it from its sleeve. She carried the arm over her own shoulder to the newsstand. "You see what sort of limbs your living person has." She showed Jacob the smooth wooden ball that had fit into the mannequin's shoulder socket.

"You didn't show me that last night," Jacob insisted. "It must have been the living one then."

Mr. Spangler, who had been gazing up at the chicken, lowered his head. "What's all this?" he asked the girl.

"Jacob always had this problem, even in the old country," she replied. "He thought everything should have a rational explanation. He thought that would be especially so in America. A few years here haven't cured him yet."

"So, what isn't rational?"

"He means according to 'natural' laws. He thinks we're only actors and that there's a third, living one somewhere."

"But didn't you tell him?" Mr. Spangler asked.

"We did. But now he doesn't believe us."

"Oh, you have to believe them," the agent told Jacob. Then, casually, as if to point out what Jacob had somehow missed, "They're telling you the truth. They aren't permitted to lie." As if this would settle the matter, he turned his attention again to the chicken. "Come down!" he called. The chicken settled more heavily on its perch; its claws scratched on the gas globe, it ruffled its feathers suspiciously. "I only asked for the material for half an hour," Mr. Spangler explained in his creaky, worried voice. "The Illusions Office doesn't like it when it comes back on its own." He made a motion toward the top hat, which suddenly vanished. "That's one at least," he said. "If I can only get the chicken down now; I'll have to give up on the rabbit."

Mr. Spangler noticed how Jacob was staring at the table where the top hat had been. "I also cure the blind," he said, as if this were a lesser thing to do. "In fact, I'm getting behind on that. I saw some blind people here the other day."

He was right there (Mr. Eisbein said); Times Square always had some blind beggars, one on every corner. There are fewer of them now; they're afraid of being mugged. Jacob was very fond of Felix, a pale, shy man who had lost his sight in a fire. Now he carved and peddled wooden trinkets: monkeys, squirrels, sea horses. He often stopped by the newsstand, where Jacob would read to him. Felix was blind indeed: Jacob had been struck with pity by his scarred face and burnt-out sockets, but he was sure that some of the other beggars were frauds, that sharp eyes lurked behind their dark glasses.

One such was approaching now, a tall, burly man with an ingratiating, bullying manner and a long green scarf. Little Green Patrick, as he was called, had a knack of pinning against a wall anyone unwary enough to stop. He would thrust his great paunch forward and tap with a white cane on one side, then the other, of his victim. He carried a bundle of white, chewed pencils in one hand, but if you tried to touch one after yielding up a coin, Patrick would squeeze the bundle tighter and snarl.

As Little Green Patrick drew near enough for Jacob to see the grease from his breakfast around his mouth, Mr. Spangler rose, straightened his shoulders with some ceremony, and pointed his finger at the beggar. Little Green Patrick's step became cautious. "For the love of God and Jesus," he said in a piteous but sturdy voice, "help a poor blind man!"

Mr. Spangler put down his finger, looked closely at the beggar, and then, arms akimbo, strode up to the big man. "Why, you scoundrel!" he exclaimed. "You're a fraud, sir, a swindler!"

The beggar stopped, drew himself up, and growled, "Out of me way, me boyo! Do you want a kick where it hurts?" He stepped forward and raised his cane, as if to strike the short, stout man who stood directly before him. Mr. Spangler raised his hand. Before his direct gaze, the beggar's cane froze in the air. Slowly he lowered it. All pretence of blindness was gone now; his voice was reasonable and humble. "I wasn't doing any harm, sir. You shouldn't interfere with the business of an honest man, or any man." He turned and walked away.

Mr. Spangler scratched his head. "And what are you doing to *my* business?" he called. He looked around Times Square again. Another beggar, wrapped in a plaid blanket, sat with a basket of wormy apples before the Times Building. Mr. Spangler examined this one carefully, then shook his head again. "Are they all fakes?" he muttered.

Then he smiled. Blind Felix, a tray of carvings round his neck, his worn face lit by the pale sunlight, tapped his way up Broadway toward the newsstand. His cane's tip found its accustomed landmarks: a lamppost, a broken bit of curb, a long crack in the sidewalk. Mr. Spangler looked at Felix calmly for a full minute, then pointed his finger.

"Ah!" Felix cried. He stepped back. His cane rose in the air, his tray tipped back, all the carved figures fell to the sidewalk. The chicken, attracted by the small objects, flew down to peck among them. Hurriedly Mr. Spangler pointed his finger again; the chicken vanished.

But no one else noticed this. Felix had bent automatically to retrieve his carvings. First, he felt with his hands as he would have done before. Then he sat back on his heels and *looked* at the figures. One by one, joyfully, he picked them up, his hand going to the right place each time. He continued as if in a trance, till the last figure was in his tray. Then he rose, hooked the cane to his elbow, and walked straight to the newsstand.

"I can see, Jacob," he whispered, as if his sight might leave if he spoke louder. "It's impossible: I can see!"

Felix removed his dark glasses. He had worn these before, not only as a sign of his condition, but to spare others the sight of his burnt, empty eyeballs. Now Jacob saw two clear green eyes looking at him in wonder.

"So that's what you're like, Jacob," Felix said. "I tried to imagine your face from your voice. Somehow, I thought you'd be bigger. How could this have happened?"

Jacob closed his eyes. When he opened them, Felix was still looking at him, out of a face scarred with the old fire. Apparently Mr. Spangler's terms of reference extended no further than the eyes. Jacob pointed to the agent. "Ask that gentleman there," he replied in a barely audible voice. "He seems to be responsible. And the others are friends of mine from the old country, Simon and Esther. They came especially to visit me." Felix blinked at them and bowed. The dancers returned his bow respectfully.

"The other one is a mannequin," Jacob continued. "They use him in their act. Now you can watch it too."

Felix stood upright, then began to back away, fearful of intruding. He kept his shining new eyes on them all as long as possible.

Esther walked to the newsstand. "Welcome again, Jacob," she said. Then she added a little sadly, "But couldn't you have believed me from the first? Why did you need a miracle to convince you?"

7

I remember now," Grandfather said. "I read about those cures of blindness. When I had the store in Bridgeport, some china came wrapped in a New York paper three years old. My wife pointed it out to me: we were both hungry for news of the city. 'Miracles on Broadway,' the item said. The reporter treated it like a joke. City air is cleaner than we thought; it has unsuspected healing powers, the paper said; three beggars who had claimed to be blind could now see. I thought, the air is cleaner in Bridgeport, but you wouldn't expect any miracles there; you wouldn't even expect any stories about miracles. I must have been more homesick than I thought."

"It did make the news," Mr. Eisbein said. "There were some real cures, and the fakes were driven away. Only one 'blind' beggar was left three months later, Leonard the Skeleton, who could see better than you or I. He had followed the sun to Mexico, as he did every winter. So he was gone while this Mr. Spangler was there. When he came back, he had the whole square to himself."

Mr. Eisbein shook his head. "Why didn't I make the connection? I once saw Mr. Spangler myself, when Jacob was still in the newsstand, but how could I take him seriously? He looked like a hundred other agents, a pale frog behind a big black desk. Why should I think he was an angel?"

"An angel?" Paul asked. "Did he have wings?"

"Of course not," Mr. Eisbein replied. "He didn't need wings."

"The angel on the Christmas tree had wings," Paul said.

"What's this about Christmas trees? In your home?" Grandfather interrupted. "No, I better not ask. Anyway, 'angel' isn't the right word. It's better to say 'messenger,' a messenger from heaven. Sometimes they say 'a man.'"

Mr. Eisbein shrugged. "So let it be 'man' or 'messenger.' This was a very anxious messenger. When I saw him, he didn't seem to be sure where he was and what he was doing.

"Let me tell you about that visit. I was very friendly then with a young lady who had theatrical ambitions, and some modest success. At that time she was with a small troupe playing supper theatre in Connecticut, on Long Island Sound. She had asked me to look around for a new agent while she was out of town. Just by chance, or so I thought, I saw the name Stephen Spangler on an office building, listed as a theatrical agent.

"The door was open, I walked in, and there was Mr. Spangler talking into a strange telephone, all gold and silver. I thought it was fake, of course; later, I wasn't sure. Where could it have been connected to? Also, now I recall, I was surprised to hear him talking Hebrew. He was saying, 'Yes, Excellency, but consider my reputation, my dignity. The landlord threatens to padlock my door if I don't pay.' Then he listened. 'Yes, of course I could make the padlock vanish,' he said, 'but what good would that do? Next, he'd send the police. The Boss explicitly told me to avoid the police.' Again he listened. 'You are certain the money will be here tomorrow? No, your word is enough. The landlord? I'll keep away from him this evening. He'll do nothing till tomorrow.' He hung up and said to me, in English, 'An important conference.' He asked me my business.

"So I showed him my friend's file of photographs, and while he examined them I looked round his office. This one had the standard furniture: a wide desk, a filing cabinet, a table covered with scripts, a bookcase with shiny titles. All a bit too new, except for the scripts. These were faded and in many languages, some of which I didn't recognize.

"As in all agents' offices, the walls were covered with pictures, but most were too dark for me to make out the faces. Only one or two seemed familiar: there was Shakespeare's face, and Molière's, as I had seen them in old prints. Then I realized that these were *photographs*. While I was trying to figure out where he had got them, Mr. Spangler finished looking at my friend's portfolio.

"He matched the fingers of both hands together and studied them. Then he picked up his telephone and spoke into it, very softly. He cleared his throat and nodded for me to come to the front of his desk. He said, 'Your friend is certainly attractive; but she will soon be leaving the theatre. Pity.'

" 'Why so?' I asked.

" 'She will meet a druggist in New London. On this very tour, in fact.' I hadn't told him my friend was touring in Connecticut. 'He is thinking of her now,' Mr. Spangler said. 'In time, he will come to the city and marry her.'

"I decided to humor him. 'She gets plenty of proposals in these small cities,' I said. 'You know, the glamour of the stage. We laugh at them together.'

" 'Not this one,' Mr. Spangler said. 'A determined, responsible man. She misses that in you now; she will miss it more in the future. Eventually, she will marry him.' Then he looked up at the ceiling as if he were listening to someone. 'Three; five,' he said. Then he added, 'She will have three children. She will outlive you by five years.' "

Grandfather asked, "Did she do what he said?"

"She did indeed marry the druggist, and she did have three children. For the rest, of course, I can't say." Then Mr. Eisbein added in mild satisfaction, "She's outlived the druggist by ten years so far."

Mr. Eisbein's eyes shone suddenly, as if a light had just gone on inside his skull. "I remember now," he said, "when I was in the office the telephone rang again. Such a sound, like silver bells in a great empty space! This time Mr. Spangler spoke in Yiddish. He was probably dealing with someone at a lower level. 'All right,' he croaked, 'you're on: Orion against the Pleiades. Even odds that Franz Ferdinand doesn't go to Sarajevo. Two to one that Princip doesn't show up. Three to one that if he does show, the Serbs and the Austrians will come to terms.' He listened and added, 'You're too pessimistic, my friend,' before he hung up.

"At the time, none of it made sense to me. I thought he was talking about some racing syndicate. Do *you* understand it?" Mr. Eisbein asked Paul.

"Orion and the Pleiades are stars," Paul said.

"What about the rest?"

Paul shook his head. Mr. Eisbein smiled. When he said no more, Grandfather explained: "He must have been talking about something that was going to happen a few years later: the assassination of the Archduke of Austria and his wife by a Serbian nationalist, a student named Gavrilo Princip. The Serbs and Austrians *didn't* come to terms, and soon the rest of Europe was involved. This was what started the First World War."

Paul said, "A war just because two people were killed?"

"Don't ask me to explain it," Grandfather said. "Your Mr. Spangler moved in high circles," he told Mr. Eisbein.

Mr. Eisbein said, "He didn't seem to think it was anything special. It sounded like an ordinary bet."

"So up there they amuse themselves betting on what people will do?" Grandfather asked.

"I think they bet on what all of us will do; it's a game there."

Paul tugged at Mr. Eisbein's sleeve. "What business did Mr. Spangler want to talk about with Uncle Jacob?"

"Oh, that. You remembered that? You see," Mr. Eisbein said, "how I get away from the story. Well, after the formerly blind beggar, Felix, had walked off into his wonderful new world and before the two dancers, Simon and Esther, carried the table and chairs back to the restaurant, Mr. Spangler told Jacob, 'I've wanted to meet you for a long time.'

" 'Why me?' Jacob asked.

" 'Oh, where I come from you're quite a topic of conversation,' Mr. Spangler said. 'They take a lively interest in your future. And now I want to look around the city, around Times Square. I'll stay here a few days, with my clients. This is the center of the world, after all, the focus of everyone's desires, what your friends always wanted. Perhaps I'll stay here, perhaps we'll all stay here. But don't mind us; just go on looking after your newsstand. You won't even know we're around.' "

Paul nodded. "Did he show Jacob how to do tricks?"

"What tricks? Card tricks?"

"Not those!" Paul replied scornfully. "Tricks like the two dancers could do."

"You'll see what tricks he showed him," Mr. Eisbein said.

Grandfather had been thinking of something else. "What kind of name is that, Stephen Spangler?"

"That wasn't the original name," Mr. Eisbein said. "The lettering on the glass of his office door had been changed. Before, it was 'Shternen Shpringer.' That means 'star-jumper' in Yiddish," he told Paul. "Maybe in another form he leaped from star to star, though you wouldn't have thought it to look at him. He must have decided to Americanize his name."

8

Even though Mr. Spangler seemed to expect Jacob to stay at his newsstand (Mr. Eisbein said), he himself suggested a day or so later that the newsdealer and his friends take the afternoon off and go sightseeing.

This was really the first time in a while that Jacob would be alone with the dancers. Though he had seen and sometimes spoken to Simon and Esther since their last meeting, Mr. Spangler had been there too, and so had thousands and thousands of others.

For New York had suddenly become aware that Christmas was near. Everyone crowded into the city to watch it arrive. The high walls of the narrow crosstown streets were splashed with bright sales advertisements. Crèches and tinseled snow appeared in the shop windows. In Macy's window, where the three mannequins had stood, a massive Santa now rocked back and forth and beat his own belly. He was so heavy and solid that probably even Mr. Spangler could not have stolen him.

Times Square blossomed. Wreaths hung from every telephone pole. Tin cutouts of Santa and the angels dangled from wires strung across the two wide streets. Colored electric bulbs ran up and down the Times Building. Wherever you looked, Santa Clauses stamped their feet and rang bells to collect for good causes. The regular beggars scowled and spat at them. All the ladies wore green and red brooches: miniature holly leaves and berries. Above these, their mouths were white and pinched and cold.

Yes, it was very cold, the coldest winter in years. Little snow had fallen, but somehow ice formed on every shaded spot. There were many comical falls. Jacob turned up his kerosene heater and counted out his papers with gloved hands. The silent Gonzalo was kept so busy handing out bags of hot chestnuts and making change that his own hands froze.

But the cold did not stop the theatres from putting on their traditional Christmas parades. Floats representing Santa's Workshop, the Three Kings at the Manger, or Dickensian Yuletide scenes criss-crossed the streets around Times Square, or rolled down Broadway to the Battery. The floats were so wide that often they could not pass each other. When a jam occurred, the drivers shouted and exchanged curses, and often the actors on the floats joined in. At Broadway and 34th Street, humble shepherds armed with crooked staffs and Santa and his elves with toy wooden swords fought a bloody battle. At Seventh Avenue and 41st Street, Tiny Tim from one float broke the nose of Bob Cratchit from another with an icicle.

The New York Theatre, where *The Sands of Guantanamo Bay* was still playing to packed houses, avoided such unseemly incidents by parking its float, of a serious, uplifting nature, on the street right before its marquee.

This was not really legal, but because of the float's religious theme, no one objected. Sergeant O'Toole even walked his dancer over to see it between her own rehearsals; she was less impressed with it than he.

On the float was a narrow white church with a baroque Spanish steeple. Before the church, American soldiers, Spanish soldiers, and humble Cuban peasants knelt together in prayer, while from the steeple electric bells beat out discreet Christmas carols. The message of the float was clear enough: reconciliation even in time of war, but in case anyone had missed it, a banner along the church's portal bore the words "The Prince of Peace Calls a Truce."

The thick crowd, which heaved and pushed to see the float, gazed with serious faces. Most women had tears in their eyes, and even men were not ashamed to show their emotions.

It was a good time for beggars, at least for some. Many people dropped coins into the apron of a short, slight woman who wore a thick shawl spotted with cornflowers. Jacob thought he had seen her before: at least, her golden hair and mild eyes, blue as the cornflowers, were very familiar. When she stopped before his newsstand, he was not surprised to hear her speak Polish.

"So many newspapers," she said. "People use them to keep warm. They shove them under their shirts and down their trousers."

Jacob said, "Do you want some? I have them from yesterday, behind the counter."

"No, no," the woman said. "I was lucky: I had my warm shawl when I made my journey." She lowered her voice. "And my woollen underdrawers and vest."

"Perhaps your friends could use the papers?" Jacob suggested.

The woman shook her head. "We came dressed as we were: some warmer, some colder. Some were only in thin nightgowns. Some had torn all the clothes off because of the fever; they were the coldest of all. You should always dress warmly before a journey!"

Then the woman smiled apologetically, a person shy of giving advice. She drifted back into the crowd, but Jacob saw her watching him anxiously, as if to tell him to dress warmly. What had happened to this poor woman, he wondered, to so derange her mind? He was glad when a child put a coin into her hand.

Other beggars fared less well. The hawk-faced man was too arrogant: it was the season for humility. The dumpy woman with the cloth bags and her little group of beggars were well organized: they divided their work so that no prosperous person would be approached too often. But they didn't do so well, either; the public sensed the conspiracy and turned away.

They were suspicious, both the public and the police, of anything out of the ordinary, especially of any illegal political activity. Word was out that foreigners had crossed the ocean to make trouble. Anarchists and socialists often appeared in newspaper cartoons; funny-looking men with beards and bombs. The anarchists were against all forms of government, which they thought only existed to repress people. They had the notion that if they caused enough disturbances, say by setting off bombs here and there, governments would collapse and we'd enter a wonderful time when everyone would live together without rules, only love and goodwill. The socialists wanted to have more government, but one in which "the people" were the real rulers. Good luck to all of them (Mr. Eisbein said)!

The police were especially concerned lest such people disturb the festive season. They had reason to worry: just the year before, two misguided young men had prepared a bomb to use against the authorities, who had refused permission for an illegal socialist demonstration. Fortunately, the young men themselves had been blown up.

The police were worried, too, that the city's poor would come swarming to the bright lights from their crowded tenements and from the shanty towns in the north of the island.

Constable Tertis growled about this one evening near Jacob's newsstand. He and another constable were looking through the window of Rector's restaurant, where a celebrated gourmet was establishing a new record in swallowing raw oysters. The oyster shucker and two waiters, as well as the patrons of the neighboring tables, watched him with growing respect.

"There's fifty of 'em, and he's still going strong," said Constable Tertis. He glowered at two shabbily dressed boys till they moved away from the window. "All the rats are coming out of their holes to watch the fun," Constable Tertis said. "We'll be ready for them. We'll give them a Merry Christmas!"

It was just as well that Constable Tertis was not present at the incident that occurred the next morning by the float in front of the New York Theatre. While the bells of the little Spanish church were chiming a slow hymn, the dancers approached. Simon was dressed in a priest's black robe, Esther as a peasant woman with red skirt and black shawl. Between them they carried the third one, the mannequin, dressed as a poor peasant, dead, with a bandage on his head and a bloody wound on his breast. They laid him on the street, directly opposite the church door. The priest stood at his head, the peasant woman at his feet.

The small crowd that was watching at that moment hummed with surprise. Others gathered to watch. But their pious faces soon grimaced with displeasure. Clearly, they found the new display morbid and in poor taste. The manager of the float — dressed as an American colonel — hissed furiously at the dancers, "Get that *dreck* out of here!" His assistant, who wore an altar boy's costume, joined him, flapping at the dancers with his wide white sleeves. The dancers bowed politely, but stayed put. The altar boy leaped down from the stage and advanced on them. When the dancers did not retreat, he fell back a step, picked up a frozen horse-dropping, and hurled it at them. It flew over their heads, into the crowd, which now joined in. They threw pine cones from their wreaths, two hard-boiled eggs, crumpled Christmas wrapping paper. Most of these missed the dancers but struck the float. Another horse-dropping stuck on the church steeple. The crowd burst out laughing; now they began to pelt the church itself.

The colonel leaped down from the stage and advanced on the dancers, clapping his hands together and stamping his feet as if to tread them down.

Sergeant O'Toole, who had approached quietly, rode Fergus between the colonel and the dancers. He looked down sternly. "That's not allowed," he told the dancers.

"What's not allowed?" Esther asked. The sergeant pulled on his mustache as if he should give this question serious thought, but before he could answer, Mr. Spangler called from near Jacob's newsstand, "Come back, now; come back here."

His voice had an unusual carrying power. He didn't have to speak again. The colonel halted, looked as if he would like to say something to Mr. Spangler, then thought better of it. The dancers picked up the mannequin. They raised him playfully as if he had only been pretending to be dead, and made him skip briskly back to the newsstand. The crowd drifted away

76

from the float. The altar boy scurried into the theatre for a ladder and brush to clean the steeple.

The dancers stood abashed under Mr. Spangler's gaze. "I *would* have to draw the troublemakers," he said. "What have I done that they should give me the troublemakers?" He shook his head. "Take the rest of the day off," he said. "You too," he told Jacob.

"I have to look after the newsstand," said Jacob.

"*I'll* look after the newsstand," Mr. Spangler replied.

Jacob was uneasy. "It's not quite as simple as it looks."

"For me it will be simple. Why shouldn't I run a newsstand? Your customers will never have seen such a newsstand."

This hardly reassured Jacob, but he only said, "You told me I should stay here."

"And now I'm telling you to go," Mr. Spangler said. "Go with your friends."

"But what shall we do, Mr. Spangler?" Esther asked.

"Do? What people do on vacation. See the sights. Take a carriage ride in the park. Visit the Statue of Liberty. Yes," he said, brightening up. "That's what you should do: see the Statue of Liberty."

The dancers seemed pleased with this suggestion, but sad too. "We always talked about seeing the Statue of Liberty before," Esther said softly. "We thought we would all see it together, Jacob."

"But you must have seen it when you came here," Jacob said. "All of us saw it from the boat. How could you enter New York harbor without seeing it?"

"We came by another way, Jacob," Esther replied.

Later that day Esther and Simon spoke of their voyage to America. They were all sitting in the enclosed lower deck of an excursion boat that cruised from Battery Park to the Statue of Liberty. At first, when the boat set out, they had stood on the upper deck together. Esther walked round the deck with Jacob, as frisky as any girl on a holiday with her special friend. She clapped her hands at the city skyline and the great liners leaving the harbor. Simon seemed happy too, and stayed discreetly a few steps behind them. Jacob's eyes shone, but when he turned round to smile at Simon his lips and nostrils had gone white. Of course, he couldn't stand the cold like the dancers, who didn't feel it at all. When Simon pointed this out to his sister, the pleasure left Esther's face. She looked at Jacob, impatient, then tender and solicitous. They went into the enclosed deck.

(Paul touched Mr. Eisbein's arm. "Was the third one with them too?" he asked.)

The mannequin was indeed with them (Mr. Eisbein said). Jacob had wanted to leave it behind, but Mr. Spangler had turned down his timid suggestion that it stay in the newsstand. "That's stolen property!" he said indignantly. "Besides," he added, leafing through the different papers with interest, "I have to mind the shop; I mustn't be disturbed."

So the mannequin came along, looking exceptionally foolish in a light spring topcoat, with a red, white, and blue band round its straw hat. Simon leaned it against a funnel of the upper deck, and when they went inside propped it between two stacks of life preservers. The mannequin would have drawn more attention from most passengers, but their fellows were an excited bunch of Russians in heavy overcoats and fur hats, who had just received their citizenship papers and were celebrating by a trip to the Statue of Liberty. They crowded to the forward windows to watch for it, exclaiming with pleasure whenever the ship struck a block of ice.

Two of my cronies were there as well (Mr. Eisbein said), also wearing fur hats like the Russians: Ewigleben, the life-insurance salesman, who had a great feeling for the important events in a man's career; and Krebs, the bad-debt collector, a stout, inconspicuous man who saw and heard everything, and who was keeping an eye on one of his "customers."

When they were halfway across, Jacob blinked at the bright water and asked, in a low voice, "Was it very bad for you?"

Esther understood immediately. "When we were sick? When our bodies died, Jacob? Yes, very bad at first. My tongue was as dry as a brick; all my skin seemed ready to tear itself away from my body. A great force was pressing on me from all sides, and as great a force was pressing out from within. The light shone so in my eyes that I knew it was saying farewell. I missed you terribly, Jacob." Here Esther laid her hand lightly on Jacob's, then withdrew it.

"I felt I had already possessed all that might have been, but then lost it," she said. "I knew that Simon was near by, that he was as sick as I. Even if he recovered, I knew his life was over — the soldiers would find him. I thought, I have brought him to this."

"And I too," Simon said. "I won't go into my own symptoms, or my thoughts of Esther or of you. I had other thoughts, which were completely irrational. I kept thinking, 'I've abandoned my comrades in the army.'"

"Comrades!" Jacob said.

"Yes, that was the word. You can imagine, I had never worried about those 'comrades' before. Then the words 'This play is over' kept repeating themselves in my mind. The light flashed in my eyes, then grew gray and dim. The words sounded themselves wearily, for the last time, 'This play is over.'

"Then someone cleared his throat and a voice announced, 'This play is over; another play is about to begin.'

"At first, I was more struck by the tone of that voice than by the words. It sounded like an anxious carnival barker, a person pushing something in which he has little confidence. I opened my eyes. I was standing in mist, in a place I could just recognize as the circle of houses round the pond in our village. People were passing on the other side of the pond, talking to each other. They seemed small and frightened. I couldn't hear their footsteps or their voices.

"But there were figures closer, whose voices I could hear. Fertig the beggar was there, talking to Simple Wanda."

"To Simple Wanda!" Jacob exclaimed. "Not the washer-woman?"

"Who else? I had heard before that she wouldn't look out for herself, that she had insisted on providing the sick with clean linen, that she had fallen sick too. I knew then that she had died."

Tears sprang to Jacob's eyes. Wanda had been a Polish woman, poor, illiterate, with kind cornflower-blue eyes and a golden heart. She had so admired learning that she thought it a privilege to clean the clothes of those who could read and write. She sang while she worked; the little children used to call out happily when they saw her coming. She had never said a cruel word about another human being.

Simon nodded while Jacob wiped his eyes. "I felt it too," he said, "the pity that such a good person should die. But I couldn't cry. I wanted to cry, but the tears wouldn't come. That was when I first truly realized I was dead.

"Then I saw Mr. Spangler, just as you've seen him, except that he wore a cloth cap. He kept pulling this off, looking at it doubtfully and putting it on again. 'Where's that girl?' he said. 'We have to get the act together. It's time to get the show on the road.' I realized that he was the owner of the carnival-barker's voice.

"I saw Esther then, sitting on the rock in the middle of the pond, testing the texture of the water with her foot. It didn't surprise me that her foot wouldn't go in. Mr. Spangler beckoned to her with a jerk of his finger. I was worried: Esther was never a girl you could order about. She looked as if she wanted to tell him so. But she stood up and walked across the water. The water didn't tremble as she passed, and she cast no shadow, but small fish swam under her feet, looking up. I watched her; I was ready to stop her before she said anything rash. Sometimes I had to do that, you'll remember. But now she just seemed curious.

"Mr. Spangler was looking in a small notebook. 'The courts are ready,' he announced. 'The advocates and judges are waiting.' He began to point around the square. 'This one goes above,' he said, looking at Simple Wanda. 'This one too,' he added, shaking his head doubtfully at Fertig.

"Then Mr. Spangler looked carefully at me. 'You stay on earth,' he said. He looked at his book, and looked at Esther, very thoughtfully. 'You can go.' He peeped at her, at the desolation in her eyes. He shrugged, spread out his hands, and added casually, 'Or, if you prefer, you can stay?' Esther nodded, unable to speak. 'Then you can stay,' he said.

"He was kind then," Simon told his sister.

She shook her head shortly. "He wanted me to stay all along; he had planned it that way. He had his reasons. He still does."

Simon looked pained at his sister's remark. "Whatever the reasons, we were able to stay together," he said gently.

"That's true," she admitted.

Her brother continued his story. "I asked Mr. Spangler then: 'Do we stay here?'

" 'Not here!' he answered. 'Not in this dump, if you'll pardon the expression. I have been in Nineveh, in Jerusalem, in York, in Toledo, in Rome. How could I stay here? No.' He looked at his book again. 'Your interest in the New York stage has been noted. For that—and for other reasons—you are to go to New York. Your sister may accompany you, while you are forced to stay on earth.'

" 'Forced to stay?' I asked. 'Is it a punishment?'

" 'Not too heavy a one, I hope.' Mr. Spangler looked embarrassed.

" 'For what sin?' I asked.

"Mr. Spangler studied his book again. 'For an unorthodox action that disturbs the moral balance of the universe. Just a little, just a very little. You abandoned your post; you deserted from the army.' "

(Here Grandfather made a face and almost interrupted. But he let Mr. Eisbein continue the story.)

"I told him," Simon said, " 'I was *inducted* into the army; I was forced to go.'

" 'You swore an oath,' Mr. Spangler replied.

" 'But what else could I do?' I asked.

"Mr. Spangler looked at me, then at his book again. 'You did swear an oath,' he repeated. 'But don't complain. You wanted to go to America; so let's go.' "

(Grandfather could no longer keep silent. "What are you saying?" he demanded. "There was something wrong in deserting from *that* army?" "Who said 'wrong'?" Mr. Eisbein asked. "You said it wasn't moral," Grandfather replied indignantly. "Are you telling me it was wrong to desert from the *Tsar*'s army?" "Not *wrong*, but apparently it upsets the balance," Mr.

Eisbein said mildly. "According to the story, poor soldiers are expected to stay where fate puts them. He is a God of battle, after all." Grandfather shook his head. Once or twice he muttered, "To say it's wrong to desert from the *Tsar*'s army!")

After Jacob had heard this much of Simon's story (Mr. Eisbein continued), he also asked, "So he brought you to America, just the two of you?"

"That's how it was planned," Simon answered, "but then other things began to happen. During this time, Fertig the beggar had been saying something to Simple Wanda. Now she opened her hand, and we saw she held two ten-zloty coins. These must have been put on her eyes, after she died.

" 'Those coins,' Fertig said.

" 'Yes, Pan Schnorrer,' Wanda answered respectfully."

("*Pan* Schnorrer!" Grandfather shook his head. He looked at Paul. " 'Pan' is 'Mister' in Polish, a title of respect. Do you know what a schnorrer is? It's a beggar who doesn't beg; one who makes you think he's doing you a favor." Paul nodded. "That's what Daddy called Mother's cousin, Albert," he said. "Never mind," said Grandfather.)

" 'Those coins,' Fertig said. 'Do you realize their significance, my good woman?'

" 'Wanda looked at her hand. 'To keep the eyes closed?' she asked timidly. 'So they shouldn't stare at people?'

" 'They are a holdover from pagan times,' Fertig told her. 'Those coins are to pay Charon the ferryman to take you across the Styx, the river of the dead.'

"Wanda seemed very impressed. 'Is that so?' she asked.

" 'Great scholars have written it,' said Fertig. 'So of course you won't need them.'

" 'Why not?' Wanda looked frightened for the first time. 'Won't Pan Charon take me?' she asked.

"Fertig said, 'You won't need him at all. As a good Catholic you don't believe in such pagan nonsense.'

" 'I don't?' Wanda seemed disappointed.

"Fertig said, 'Of course you don't! An angel will come for you, one with a trumpet and wings, and gold trimming. He should be here already.'

"Wanda looked around, but saw no such angel. She walked toward Mr. Spangler and asked, without any confidence, 'Is it you, Pan?'

" 'Who, me?' Mr. Spangler said. 'Hardly!' He looked in his book. 'I have you here for cross-reference only,' he said, 'but you're not one of mine.'

" 'Your own angel will come,' Fertig said. 'Everything is arranged; your Book says so. Your future is all taken care of. But what will become of me?'

"Wanda looked at him with compassion. 'Do you need the coins, Pan?' she asked.

"Fertig said, 'Who can tell? Who knows what rivers I have to cross? Without a coin I might wander forever, lost among criminals and monsters, among those who could choose neither good nor evil.' You'll remember that Fertig was always something of a freethinker, a man who read everything. Perhaps he regretted it now, though not very much.

"Then Wanda's kind blue eyes looked very sad indeed. She would have cried, if the dead were able to cry. 'Here, Pan Schnorrer,' she said, 'you take the money.'

"But just as Fertig was reaching out for the coins," Simon said, "Fat Bella, who used to sell hot corn gruel and who had come up in time to hear this conversation, thrust herself between them. She shouted at Fertig, 'Shame on you! Shame on you! I always knew you were a crook. That snooty air of yours never fooled me! Didn't I always say you'd steal the coins from a corpse's eyes? And now you're doing just that!'

"Fertig drew himself up. 'Stealing!' he said. 'Never in my past life did I take what wasn't freely given!'

" 'He can have them! He can have them, Panni Bella,' Wanda said. 'I want him to have the money.'

"Fat Bella ignored her. 'It's bad luck!' she cried. 'You shouldn't look at dead people; you shouldn't touch them; you shouldn't think of them. And now you want her coins!'

"Mr. Spangler put his peaked cap back on his head and clapped his hands together. 'Stop this quarreling,' he said. 'You're giving me a headache.'

" '*You* have a headache?' Fat Bella said. '*I* had a headache!

My head, my elbows, the soles of my feet, other parts I won't mention, how they all ached! They're aching again, now that I think of it!'

"Then," said Simon, "I saw something black approaching rapidly through the mist. Reb Nahum came striding up, leading the way with his pointed beard, just as he did when he was alive. In fact, I kept watching him to see if his mouth would drop open. Do you remember?" Simon asked Esther.

Esther smiled: she remembered, and so did Jacob. Every now and then, Reb Nahum would say a sensible or even a clever thing. When this happened, he was so surprised that his mouth fell open and stayed open for a few moments, so that his red gullet shone between his black beard and his mustache.

"But it didn't happen this time," Simon continued. "Reb Nahum called out, 'Aches and pains! Aches and pains! You can only think about your own selfish feelings! You should beat your breasts; you should cover your heads; you should beg for forgiveness!'

" 'Forgiveness!' Fat Bella said.

"Fertig sniffed and raised his sharp beak of a nose. 'Forgiveness?' he asked Reb Nahum. 'It may be the other way round, Monsieur.' Then I knew we were in for trouble: Fertig only used the title Monsieur for those he despised. He said now, 'It may be that someone should beg us for forgiveness.'

"Reb Nahum cried out, 'Blasphemy!'

"Fertig ignored him. 'For myself, I won't say,' he continued, 'but Wanda here was a truly good person, the kindest I ever knew. Even Fat Bella had no real harm in her, only foolishness. And our two young friends' — here he looked at Esther and me — 'had real talent, all wasted now. Who will answer for that?'

" 'Well, thank you very much!' Fat Bella said. Reb Nahum opened and closed his mouth three times. 'Oh, you miserable scoundrel!' he cried to Fertig. 'If only I were more intelligent, I'd make you see how wrong you are!'

" 'Please!' Mr. Spangler cried. 'Enough.'

"Then Fat Bella said, though I'm not sure who she was

speaking to, 'You wouldn't talk that way if your stomach ached like mine did. It was as big as a haystack! It was worse than childbirth!'

"Reb Nahum immediately covered his ears. 'Shameless!' he cried. 'Let me tell you, your miserable stomach was nothing compared to my eyes. They pushed themselves out of their sockets so that I could see my own skull.'

"And then," Simon continued, "Fat Bella and Reb Nahum began to trade symptoms: pains, nausea, vast depressions, lakes of red vomit, rivers of black vomit; until Mr. Spangler, who had tried to shush them and had even put his hands over his ears, beckoned to Esther and me to come closer. Then he flung his peaked hat high in the air; it landed on the roof of a house, inside an empty stork's nest. He waved his arms and cried out, 'To the New World! To New York!'

"The village vanished. Esther and I found ourselves flying somehow, high above the clouds, with Mr. Spangler in the lead. Europe passed beneath us: we saw vineyards and gray, dusty cities. Then the English Channel; England, then Ireland, and we were over the open Atlantic. But I realized that Mr. Spangler had brought others with us who should have gone elsewhere. Fertig was just behind us, and Wanda, who was close enough to him to pass him the two coins. Farther back, I heard Fat Bella say, 'Oy! I'm not standing on the ground!' And just behind her, Reb Nahum cried, '*You're* touching nothing? *I'm* standing on a void, an abyss!' Mr. Spangler looked back at them. 'Enough! Please, enough!' he cried. He looked wildly around the sky and called, 'Couldn't it have been simple, for once?'

"But apparently he couldn't send them back and they were with us all the way to the coast of America. New York City was covered with clouds; we saw nothing of it until we landed between mountains of coal by a dirty dock on the East River. Mr. Spangler had managed to lose the others in the clouds. At least, they were no longer with us."

"He didn't really lose them," Esther said. "I've seen them around."

.

"I've seen them, too," Jacob said. "I'm glad they dressed warmly," he added.

"But I don't know what they did for bodies," Esther said, looking down fondly at her own. "We took the best mannequins in the city."

9

D o you have your pills?" Grandfather asked Mr. Eisbein.

Mr. Eisbein blinked, and blinked again. "Is it time?" He felt in his jacket pocket and shook his head. "I'd better go get them."

"Stay, rest," Grandfather said. "Paul can go: he needs a run. Are they in your night table?"

Mr. Eisbein nodded. "The blue ones, like shiny eggs."

"Don't tell the story without me," Paul said.

"We won't," said Grandfather. "Mr. Eisbein will think about the next part."

Mr. Eisbein looked across the river. "Who has to think? You hurry back," he told Paul.

But Paul took longer than he wanted. He found the pills at once, but on the way back, as he passed the door to the sunroom, a sharp voice called, "Little boy!"

Paul didn't like that, but he walked into the sunroom. The tall windows on one side looked toward a busy street. Mrs. Dobin, the lady from lunch with very yellow hair, sat at a table near these windows, playing cards with a long-nosed man whose bald head was so shiny Paul could see the colors of moving cars reflected on it. The windows on the other side opened on the riverbank, where Grandfather and Mr. Eisbein sat staring across the river at the fairgrounds.

"We saw you sitting with your grandpa and his friend." Mrs. Dobin nodded toward the river. "My, Mr. Eisbein was busy talking!"

The bald man grunted. "He's a talker, all right."

"We thought he must have been telling one of his stories. Was he?" Mrs. Dobin stared at Paul hungrily and held his eyes until he muttered, "Kind of."

Mrs. Dobin clapped her hands. "He's such a storyteller! He's been everywhere and done everything! What was it this time, his casino at Saratoga Springs?"

"Ha!" the bald man remarked. "The almost-millionaire!"

Of course, Paul wasn't going to say what they had been talking about, but he didn't know how to get away. He shook his head and tried to look dumb.

"Or was it the Canadian rumrunners on Lake Memphremagog?" Mrs. Dobin asked.

The bald man said, "Lay off, Molly! Leave the kid alone."

"Oh well, I certainly don't want to pry," Mrs. Dobin said. "As long as you don't take him too seriously."

The bald man laid a lot of cards on the table. "Gin."

"Oh, you clever fellow!" Mrs. Dobin said. "I wasn't expecting that."

"You have to pay attention to the discards," the bald man said. "The main thing is to keep track of the discards. I'm a realist," he added.

"You certainly keep your eyes on the here and now," Mrs. Dobin agreed.

The bald man began dealing the cards again, but Paul didn't leave. He had started to answer Mrs. Dobin in his own mind. He realized that he *had* been taking Mr. Eisbein seriously: he had really believed him. Probably it was because Grandfather had been there too and had seemed to go along with the story. It wasn't even like the stories at summer camp round the bonfire, where the big trees and the shadows and the wood noises gave you an excuse for being scared. No, he had swallowed all that stuff in broad daylight! Paul looked out on the street side, toward the real world, where lines of cars had stopped for a red light. "Aha!" the bald man exclaimed. He made a pencil mark on a little pad. "Another Edsel!" He explained to Paul, "I have this contest with my roommate: who sees the most of one kind of car. Last week it was Rolls-Royces. I won then, too."

Mrs. Dobin said, "I think it's wonderful the way the two of you trust each other to keep score."

"If we can't trust each other, what's the sense of it all?" The bald man and Mrs. Dobin nodded together sagely. In a minute the bald man scored another Edsel.

Paul walked slowly toward the river, wondering if Mr. Eisbein would realize that he no longer believed him. He went over the story in his mind, to decide if he could believe any of it. Uncle Jacob had existed: everyone talked about him, and he had seen his picture. The family stories made sense, as Grandfather had told them, and he could even believe that Uncle Jacob had had a newsstand in Times Square. He might have known a policeman, some beggars, and several traveling salesmen. But what about the rest: the mannequins and the spirits from the old country, and the angel or messenger? Mr. Eisbein couldn't really have believed all that! He was just teasing Paul, pretending to be so serious. But was Grandfather teasing him too? He had never done so before, not in that way.

Paul came to a fork in the gravel path. The left branch led straight back to the bench; the right branch led to some thick rhododendron bushes by the river's edge. He thought that there might be another path by the bushes that would take him back to the bench. If he went round that way, he would have a little more time to think before he had to face Grandfather and Mr. Eisbein. He moved forward, his steps dragging.

Paul had taken so long to return that Grandfather and Mr. Eisbein began talking again. Grandfather asked, "And did they see the Statue of Liberty?"

"They did; they joined the other sightseers, and read the poem by Emma Lazarus at the base of the statue. You know it," Mr. Eisbein said:

" 'Give me your tired, your poor,
Your huddled masses yearning to be free,
The wretched refuse of your teeming shores.
Send them, the homeless, tempest-tossed to me.
I lift my lamp beside the golden door.' "

Grandfather nodded. "All my children had to learn it in school."

"The new citizens oohed and aahed over the poem," Mr. Eisbein continued. "But the girl, Esther, chewed the words until she had climbed to the statue's head and was looking out at the city through the openings in the crown. Then she muttered, a little too loudly, 'Wretched refuse! Wretched refuse indeed! Let her speak for herself! Our ancestors were arguing the most subtle points of the Law while theirs were using their Scripture to justify slavery!'

"None of the Russians understood her comments, but they recognized her critical tone. They began to hiss and growl among themselves, like good citizens. Esther's brother and Jacob whispered to the girl; she shrugged, but remained silent.

"On the trip back, she and Jacob sat together in the boat's bow, while her brother stayed in the stern with the mannequin. The young couple watched the skyline of the city, new skyscrapers going up everywhere. They talked together, very quietly; no one heard what they said. After they landed, they were in no hurry to return to Times Square. Jacob and the girl strolled up Fifth Avenue together looking into shop windows: furniture, drapes, books, kitchenware. At times they smiled happily, occasionally they laughed sadly, as if at some grim secret joke. Simon walked with the mannequin across the street. Someone who saw them all said that they looked like a shy couple, courting, with the girl's brother keeping his distance so that they could get closer to each other."

Across the river, the three musicians were singing, apparently, about the perils of love; though the words were not quite clear enough to hear. "Who are *they?*" Mr. Eisbein asked. "What happened to the German band?"

"Old Shemtov told me: the Germans suddenly got a big engagement in the city. This bunch just came along, he said. When it was warm yesterday his grandson, the doctor, pushed him out in the chair. Shemtov said the girl sang a kind of lullaby he had heard only his mother sing; he had thought she made it up. Shemtov said probably he was just dreaming."

Suddenly, the song from across the river became clear. One of the men, the short tenor of the group, sang:

"My love and I strolled round the village,
Hand in hand through the sweet summer meadow.
We smiled at the dolls in the cottage windows,
At the dancing bees in their sunbeam curtains.
We bowed to the great king riding by."

Then the girl and the tall man with the deep voice sang:

"Beware, beware of the witch of the meadow!
With her sharp black hat
And her cold blue eye.
She'll shred you in her scissors
With the bees and the poppies,
The plumes of the kings
And the dolls' golden tresses.
She'll weave you in her carpet of stars and sky."

On the riverbank the frogs, which had grouped themselves into a cozy circle, leaped into the water and swam away from each other.

Paul heard the song begin when he reached the riverbank, beside the thick rhododendron bushes. While it continued, he stood very still, thinking of nothing at all. As the song ended, he saw that there was no real path along the bank, only a ledge a few inches wide that might have been a path once. The current had cut into the bank at this point and the water was very deep.

Despite this, he could see right down to the bottom. It was strange that the river should be so clear. He had never been

91

able to see beneath the surface before. His father used to talk about all the dirty things that people threw into the river: by the time it reached the Hudson, you could practically walk on it.

Paul watched the river bottom near him. He could count the stones that showed above the muck, the empty cans, a few clams. He could tell which clams were alive, because their shells opened and closed, very slowly.

But even farther out he could look deeply into the water. He saw fish swimming: a stubby fish with a pouting, foolish mouth; a slim, mean fish, very powerful; a cylindrical fish whose mouth was open as wide as its body. All the fish seemed to be resting.

Paul raised his eyes to the surface again. Ten feet away, a snake was swimming, perhaps the same one that had stalked the frogs. He could see inside it. Paul blinked his eyes. It was true: the snake was transparent. Somehow the sunlight, which struck the water at a low angle as it passed over the bandstand, went right through it. The bright water around the snake dazzled Paul's eyes, but the snake's insides were cool, darker, and very clear. Paul could see how its powerful muscles were laid on top of each other. Suddenly he understood how their movement propelled the snake through the water in its peculiar zigzag pattern.

The snake must have just finished eating a frog. In its stomach, bits and pieces of its meal were slowly dissolving. Once when Paul had seen the insides of a dog crushed on the street, he couldn't eat for two days. But now he was only interested in watching the snake digest the frog. He saw — or at least he understood, he couldn't have told you how — that the snake's blood was passing through millions of little tubes by its stomach and intestines, picking up the food it was getting from the frog and carrying it throughout its long body.

If he squinted, he could see the red cells in the blood, almost like the ones he had read about in the book his mother said was too old for him, the cells that carried oxygen through the snake's body. If he looked even more closely he thought he could see the oxygen, which looked like two little balls spinning round each other. Paul blinked his eyes: this was *really* just his imagination, or the sunlight on the water! But the pairs of balls didn't vanish.

Paul stepped forward to watch more closely. A man's voice, and another one just behind it, cried, "Paul, look out!" A girl's voice repeated, "Paul, look out! Look out!" He tried to stop, but one foot was already over the edge. His momentum carried him forward. The other foot struck a crumbly bit of bank. His arms flailed as he tried to regain his balance. The first man's voice called out, "The bushes!" and a deeper voice called, "Grab behind you!" He obeyed instinctively. His hand caught a branch and he pulled himself backward into the rhododendron bush. "Oh, good!" the girl's voice said. "Good! Good!"

It was only when he had scrambled out of the bush and edged round to the side away from the water that Paul, his legs still trembling, could think about the voices. They had rung in his ears, but there had been no echo: almost as if they had sounded inside his head. The voices, especially that of the girl, had sounded so anxious, so desperate! Paul looked around for the people who had called so loudly. Only Grandfather and Mr. Eisbein were on the bench, staring across the river, not talking at all.

Paul held a thick branch and looked down toward the bank. It was really crumbly: he *would* have fallen in. Then he remembered that he couldn't swim. He had never learned. He was afraid of water. He didn't think his parents swam either; he had never seen them do it. They whispered about people who drowned, how foolish they were to swim in dangerous places. Paul thought, I have to learn how to swim, really swim. A crazy but very clear thought entered his brain from somewhere: because if I drowned, how could I tell the story? Someday, only I will know it, and it must be told.

He joined Grandfather and Mr. Eisbein on the bench. Neither one turned his head from looking across the river.

"Go on with the story," Paul said, almost rudely.

Mr. Eisbein took the pills from Paul's hand, swallowed one with the help of a little flask in his coat pocket, and began to speak.

10

ॐ

What a winter that was (Mr. Eisbein said)! Snow was piled on the curbs, it melted and froze on the sidewalks. You could see old people, like your grandpa and me now, looking out of windows, afraid to go even to the store or the restaurant because of the ice; some looked pale and hungry.

By chance the small, timid beggar Sir Stefan was able to see and hear what no other person could. The basement of Rector's restaurant had recently been enlarged, and a ventilation grate through which warm air rose was placed in the sidewalk beside the newsstand. Naturally, this would attract a homeless beggar: many slept on such grates. But, even better, a few days before Christmas Sir Stefan found a large, empty china-packing box, which he installed over the grate, one side touching the news-stand. He patiently bored holes in the bottom of his box to let the warm air in and found an old blanket, which he slit down the middle, for a front door.

The day he installed the box, Sir Stefan worked as never in his life. By evening it was covered with discarded Christmas wrapping paper. He had even found a small statue of Santa Claus for the top, which gave the box such a festive air that no one thought of moving it. Sergeant O'Toole, who had watched the little beggar scurrying to construct this nest, looked away every time he passed it. At least the beggar would be safe this winter: his would not be one of the stiff derelict bodies the sergeant found each winter, after they had said a silent farewell to the hard streets.

Sir Stefan's food supply was plentiful too. Moved by the bountiful season, the restaurant customers ordered more than they could eat, and the garbage cans were full. Tiny Sir Stefan became so chubby that he had trouble squeezing in through the narrow slit in his blanket. At night he dreamed of spring and warm autumns. He remembered the sunlight in an apple orchard where he had once found work as a young man, and had been as quick and neat as any of the other pickers.

He worried sleepily about his shelter, which he knew could not survive the post-Christmas clean-up. But perhaps Jacob could be persuaded to build it onto his newsstand, say as a place to store extra papers, with a bit of room for a homeless beggar. Normally, Sir Stefan would already have discussed this with Jacob, but the newsdealer was changed, quiet and withdrawn. He paid no attention to the weather. One evening, snow blew in on his head and seemed to remain a long time afterward. Then Sir Stefan realized that much of Jacob's hair had gone white.

And his face had changed too; he no longer watched the street with such bright eyes. Instead, he seemed to be looking at things far away: those in the sky, perhaps, or those within himself that were even farther. Once, Sir Stefan remembered, Jacob had had a special look for each passerby, an eager sympathy, a curiosity for the story behind each new face. Now, the only thing that really roused the newsdealer was the sight of the two dancers, the boy and the girl, who once said strange words to Sir Stefan; the ones who always carried a dummy with them, a dummy that they made take part in their dances in such a clever way that you could almost swear it was alive.

The beggar saw that Jacob's face lit up when these three passed, and his eyes followed them hungrily down the street. Whenever the dancers talked to Jacob, a jolly fat man would stand near them, smiling. But in the last week before Christmas, the dancers had avoided the newsstand altogether.

Once or twice, when they seemed about to approach, the fat man had come between them and the newsstand and, hands crossed behind his back, had stared up at the sky till the dancers left.

But Sir Stefan had other concerns to occupy him now: some trouble was in the air. The other beggars of Times Square kept whispering to each other. They gathered in groups of two or three; sometimes a small crowd formed, then dispersed quickly if a policeman looked that way. Sir Stefan stayed away from these gatherings. He was a loner; he had always worked only for himself. He was sure that if he joined forces with another beggar he would lose by it. Once or twice, indeed, when he had fainted from hunger, other beggars had asked for money on his behalf. But he had not got any of the money, and no more food than a stale doughnut.

Still, some of the whispers reached him. He heard one strange warning: "Be ready for the dance." And one stranger still: "Those who are going to be happy can wait a little."

Christmas came on a Monday that year. Sir Stefan finally learned that on Saturday night, when the late shops and the theatres closed, the beggars of Times Square planned to dance in a line across the downtown end of the square so as to prevent anyone from leaving. Or at least to make them "wait a little." The beggars had caught the idea, perhaps from the air, that if the theatregoers and last-minute shoppers were delayed on their way home to family and Christmas trees, they would not be annoyed; on the contrary, they would be amused, happy, and generous. Their hearts would grow with deeper understanding of those who had no happiness in store. They would *want* to give more.

Sir Stefan became very frightened, especially when he learned that posters and banners were being prepared. These were sure to attract the police. He thought of leaving the square altogether, but couldn't bear to abandon his cozy home. At least, he decided, he would remain well hidden. He cut out peepholes in the sides of his box in order to see without being seen.

Still, he had to get about on his own business, and while scavenging in the back alleys he saw cloth streamers being painted with the slogan "Those who are going to be happy can wait a little." This was bad enough, but even worse happened on his own doorstep. The day of the dance, the fat woman with the cloth bags and some of her beggars prepared their own signs right on Broadway, almost in front of the newsstand. Two placards, to be carried beside each other, read: "It's unlucky" and "to be happy too soon." The first sign, painted by a former carpenter who had lost his left hand in a sawmill, was blocky and workmanlike. The second, by an artist who still hoped for fame when people's fundamental values changed, was full of curlicued letters and happy bluebirds. The fat woman supervised the painting and grumbled about bad luck.

"Did you see that streetcar?" she muttered in a voice as thick as pudding. "Right on the back it had an advertisement for tea next to one for cigarettes. Don't they know any better? That means the wheel will fall off!"

"Please, Bertha!" the former carpenter objected. "By you, everything is an omen."

"I know what I'm talking about," the fat woman insisted. "Such a thing happened to a streetcar just past the Brooklyn Bridge." Then she waved her finger at Jacob, who sat as if frozen in his newsstand. "Even in America the laws must be obeyed!"

"What laws?" the artistic beggar asked.

"The laws that say one thing means another." The fat woman spoke as if this should have been obvious to anyone. "And keep away from willow trees," she added, pointing across the street to the courtyard of The Three Knocks.

"Ha!" the carpenter replied. "Do you think we're idiots? *Everyone* knows better than to touch a willow tree. Isn't that right?" he demanded of Jacob, but the newsdealer turned his head away.

Sergeant O'Toole, with Fergus in tow, stopped by the newsstand. The great horse blew out his nostrils at the signs, as if in amazement. The sergeant shook his head. "They'd better look out," he told Jacob gloomily. "Those signs may not be illegal, but some members of the force are getting nervous. They think there's going to be a big demonstration. They're talking about anarchists, and foreign agitators, and I don't know what. I've told them, 'Nonsense! I know the beggars here. Except for a bit of innocent fraud, not an ounce of harm in the lot of them.' But I think some of my colleagues would enjoy a bit of trouble."

The sergeant had deeper reasons to be sad. His dancer would soon be leaving. A new show was to appear at the Xanadu Theatre. On very short notice, *Great Gotham Follies* was going on a nationwide tour. This could take months, years even; it was doubtful if all the members of the touring company would find work again in New York. What made it worse was that the sergeant had learned of this from others: his dancer hadn't even thought it worth her while to tell him.

But Sergeant O'Toole watched over his beat despite his heavy heart. He looked keenly around the Square. "I see some new faces here, not my regular customers," he said. "They seem to be keeping out of the light. Where do they all come from?"

Small groups of shabby men and women had drifted into the uptown end of Times Square. They looked around the strange territory and drifted out again. In a short time many had passed, all avoiding the light, as the sergeant had said. "They must be from the shanty towns," the sergeant observed. "They don't seem to be looking for peace on earth. I'd better keep an eye on them." He mounted Fergus and rode to the uptown end of the square. There, his substantial figure could be seen passing to and fro as the sun set. The black figures darted here and there so that not even his long shadow touched them. And then, as the streets grew darker, as the theatres opened and last-minute shoppers filled the stores, these mysterious figures were hidden.

This evening, the light was confused. The winds struck from every direction. The swinging signs were brighter than ever. The falling snow tossed in streamers and spirals that glittered more brightly still. When Gonzalo, the hot-chestnut vendor, beat up his fire, the sparks rushed up to escape the earth. Gonzalo watched them, shaking his head. Then, though it was still early, he crossed himself and departed, singing an old Italian Christmas carol.

The theatres emptied. Snow was falling, so erratically that sometimes only one member of a walking couple would be dusted with white. Now the shops were closing; masses of shoppers, balancing under stacks of bright parcels, pushed into streets where there was no room for them. The bodies jostled together without purpose. Then the crowd collected itself, each particle acquired a sense of direction, and opposing currents began to move to the uptown and downtown ends of the square. At this moment, the dance of the beggars started.

It began in a line, out from the alley by Rector's restaurant. Ladder Jenkins, a tall man with broad, crooked shoulders and very spindly legs, led the way, playing on a wheezy accordion "There'll Be a Hot Time in the Old Town Tonight." He was accompanied in his march and music by Lips Lannigan, a corpulent dwarf with a cornet, which, because of the cold, was a half-tone lower than the accordion.

Next came the dumpy woman whom the beggars called Bertha, followed by the former carpenter and the artist who mistakenly had their signs in reverse order: "to be happy too soon" and "It's unlucky." Felix, the once blind beggar, followed. He now made a modest living selling his carved figures to the shops, and had joined the others out of sympathy. Round his neck he carried a small basket of dancing figures, plaited from straw, which he tossed out to the crowd.

There followed short and tall beggars, bobbing unevenly to the music like gaps in a row of teeth. Two with identical height and perfect step carried the banner "Those who are going to be happy can wait a little." Shortly behind them were two sandwich-board men, one advertising a restaurant, the other a new gift shop. On the bottom of their boards, front and back, they had written, "No hurry! You'll enjoy it more if you wait." Each was followed by a beggar who, with tin cans nailed to the ends of two sticks, beat upon the sandwich boards. The sandwich-board men winced at each blow.

And behind these was Little Green Patrick, the false blind man who had been absent from Times Square ever since his meeting with Mr. Spangler but who had returned for the parade. His dark glasses were shoved up over his forehead and he twirled a green wreath on his blind man's stick.

A few beggars later, at the very end of the line, came the

Gypsy family, who appealed mainly to prosperous middle Europeans. A squat, cross-eyed woman in a black kerchief carried in her arms a baby with piercing, direct eyes, who held out a cup. The Gypsy father, whose red earrings touched his shoulders, strummed a great guitar. Tattered gloves on both his hands greatly muffled the tone, but his rhythm was perfect.

So then the beggars, some twenty-five or thirty of them, made their way in a weaving, bobbing line across Broadway. The crowd, of course, gave way. Those who had their hands free applauded. This must be the last parade of the season! Many shook their heads at the signs. One kind lady, balancing her tower of packages under an aristocratic but humane chin, asked the line at large, "Do you think you *should* wait for your happiness to come?"

Others were less concerned with the beggars' happiness, but willing enough to give them money. Small, lively beggars with red gnomes' caps darted among the crowd; each rang a bell with one hand, and held out a red bucket with the other.

As coins rang in the buckets, the musicians at the head and tail of the line changed their melody to "Molly Malone." All over the square, rich Irish voices took up the song. The line of beggars crossed Seventh Avenue, momentarily halting the traffic there, circled round, and entered Broadway again.

It was all harmless enough (Mr. Eisbein said). Anyone who wanted to get past the dancing beggars could easily do so. There was not an atom of truth in the City's official story at the judicial inquiry that the beggars had blocked the downtown exits of Times Square and kept the public hostage until they paid up. The beggars just happened to be in the wrong place at the wrong time—though maybe that's the greatest fault of all. As the last strains of "Molly Malone" died down, an angry murmur rolled in from the uptown end of the square. The crowd was clearing there, leaving a line of dark figures who stood shoulder to shoulder at the level of 47th Street.

These figures carried serious placards: "Give us work." "Decent housing." "Justice." "Living Wages." Dwellers in the shanty towns in the northern part of Manhattan Island had

chosen this night to interject their grim protest into the city's gaiety.

Of course (Mr. Eisbein said) it went over like a lead balloon. Who wanted to be bothered with such dull business at this time? The crowd fell silent. A few groaned; others whistled mockingly. Only the beggars replied. "Decent housing!" they cried. "Justice!" Their howls of derision echoed round the square.

Sensing trouble, people began to leave. They flowed round the demonstrators at one end of the square, and round the beggars at the other. But one man ran to the very center of the square, his head thrown back, his sharp, pointed beard leading his body forward. He spun round, looking first at the beggars, then at the demonstrators, so that his words were sprinkled around the square.

"Foolishness! Foolishness!" he cried. "I don't understand any of this. I know it's wrong! Why aren't you at home where you belong?"

The beggars applauded. "We are at home!" they called. "This is our home!"

The man with the pointed beard seized his head in his hands. "I don't understand." He shook his fist at the sky. "Why wasn't I made more intelligent?" he demanded. Then he turned back to the beggars. "But tell me, you wise men: did you come to America for this?" And then his mouth dropped open, his teeth shone, a blacker hole glowed between them. Jacob, the newsdealer, drew two stacks of newspapers close to his head as if for shelter.

Suddenly, all the streetlights were turned off. Many of the shop windows followed. Darkness grew in the square. Then, when the blackness seemed complete, spotlights were turned on both the beggars and the demonstrators. The protesters shut their eyes to the dazzling beam, but the beggars turned and whirled in it as in a shower of rain. Their feet threw up the snow; they danced in a field of light.

Now, from the west side of the square, at 45th Street, a whistle blew. The mellifluous official voice of the Deputy Police

Commissioner, who had once trained as an opera singer, announced on a speaking trumpet: "Clear the square! Clear the square! All persons obstructing traffic are to leave the streets immediately, following civic ordinance D 585." As the echoes of this command died down, a sharper voice added, "Get out of it, you vermin! Get off the streets, you scum!"

"Restrain yourself, Constable Tertis," the speaking trumpet admonished him. Then it added, in deeper tones, "All persons obstructing the movement of other persons are to leave the streets immediately."

At the outer fringes of the downtown spotlight a lady in a fur hat began to cry. A younger woman took her arm and led her away. The few remaining pedestrians quickly left the square. Cabs that had been lurking around the edges drove off down side streets. The beggars saw them all off with bells and cheering; the musicians played "Good Night, Ladies."

The action of the protesters at the far end of the square was more direct and purposeful. They drew together in a hard line, holding their signs like banners, then quickly filed in their line through the nearby crowd, until a mass of innocent shoppers shielded them from the spotlights. Chanting "We'll never yield to the brutal reactionaries!" they marched bravely out of sight, leaving the beggars to face the police alone.

From 45th Street a whistle blew twice. An orderly row of shapes, closely bunched at first, emerged into the light: dark blue above, brown below, a squad of mounted policemen, New York's finest. The whistle blew again. The horsemen advanced at a slow walk, spreading out into a perfect, evenly spaced line that slowly wheeled and, in beautiful order, advanced at a slow trot.

The beggars, too elated to sense their danger, stood in a line across Seventh Avenue. Many applauded. The bolder ones advanced, clapping hands or ringing bells, for a better look. Now spotlights shone from all around the square. Light reflected warmly from the snow on the horsemen's leather boot' which straightened together as each man rose in his seat ʳ the line charged the beggars.

The muscles of the young policemen bulged under their blue tunics. The steps of the sleek, strong horses were muffled. Snow rose round their feet as if they were walking on clouds. They seemed ready to leave the ground completely, to ride off into the air, between the narrow canyons of the city. On the right end of the line, proudest of all, rode Constable Tertis. He had asked for this position, "to catch any lice that try to creep away."

But don't worry (Mr. Eisbein told Grandfather, who was listening with close attention, pulling at his beard), this wasn't like the Cossacks riding down peasants. True, it started that way, but New York beggars knew how to dodge. The lame, the halt, and the blind could scuttle and scoot away from danger better than Olympic athletes. Most escaped. Some darted behind the row of garbage cans by the Times Building. They rolled two cans in front of the horses, which reared back and neighed. Three drunkards who had been dozing over a pavement grating cursed, then escaped through a dark alleyway, helped by the stream of escaping beggars.

The north wind got into the act too. It struck the man with the pointed beard so fiercely that he could not hold his ground. He fled before it; as he disappeared down Broadway his feet no longer seemed to touch the street. The wind lifted the skirts and petticoats of the fat Bertha and sent her skipping south. The shy, timid woman with cornflower-blue eyes and golden hair ran out to help hold Bertha's clothes down. Together they were blown down Seventh Avenue.

But in the open square, three beggars were trapped within a circle of horsemen. All these beggars were bearded: a tall one with a long white beard, a shorter one with a longer black beard, and a fat one with a broad red beard and completely bald head that shone as he spun between the other two, all circling to find a way out. The spotlight moved to center exactly on his bald dome. The horses reared up so that their hooves were almost level with the beggars' faces. The policemen's helmets seemed as tall as the buildings.

The police edged their horses close to the circle the moving beggars had marked out in the snow. "Dance! Dance!" the policemen cried. These riders were expert: they carried the banners in the Columbus Day parade. Their horses tripped as daintily as ballet dancers, much more daintily than the beggars. They stamped just beside the beggars' feet when the bearded men faltered. Sometimes a beggar would cry out, but the police agreed later that this was a sham. Their horses had never touched the old fakers! They were just trying to get public sympathy.

Then, just when it seemed that the dance would go on forever, a shout of many laughing voices pierced the air. The police broke their circle and turned to watch a strange sight indeed: Constable Tertis dangling and wiggling from a lamppost.

No, it wasn't all up with the Tiger of Times Square. The ardent fellow had torn himself away from the three old men to pursue a small, crooked beggar who ran down Broadway like a singed rabbit. When the beggar turned into an alley, Constable Tertis rode over the sidewalk and into a spike that supported a "No Parking" sign. The spike just missed his flesh but passed through the shoulder of his tunic. The sign clattered to the ground. His horse slipped from beneath him. The constable sagged down in his uniform; his face disappeared in his collar; his arms flew upward. The more he thrashed around, the firmer the spike was embedded in his tunic. He looked like a heavy, wet sack, bulging at the bottom.

Before the other policemen noticed Constable Tertis's predicament, one of the fleeing beggars had hung a sign on his toes: "Happiness can wait a little." Now his fellow policemen gathered around him, laughing. "Wait a little!" they joked. "Wait a little! You make such a pretty signpost!"

From black alleys beggars crept out to cheer, ready to fly on the instant. But by this time the police were tired of the excitement. They rode under Constable Tertis and freed him. He stumbled away without dignity, trying to catch his horse, which wilfully kept its distance. His fellow policemen watched without interest. Beggars whistled shrilly in derision. The police waved languid clubs; there would be no more pursuit that night.

And now the police departed, riding away with a jolly clatter. Their voices were fresh and wholesome. No one paid attention to the three dancing beggars who lay exhausted in the middle of Broadway. Soon they too rose and went their separate ways, hurrying from each other as fast as they could. The spotlights were turned off, the ordinary streetlights on. Lights began to appear again in the shop windows. Late passersby looked into the bright windows as if, and this was probably true, they had no idea of what had just occurred.

Besides Sir Stefan, only one beggar had taken no part in the parade: the hawk-faced man who always begged as if he were conferring a favor. Now he appeared from somewhere and approached the newsstand, kicking up the snow lightly. He bowed to Jacob. "Good evening, Mr. Newsdealer," he said.

Jacob nodded and opened his mouth, but did not reply. "Have you perhaps a paper for me?" the beggar asked.

Jacob pointed to his stacks of papers and looked questioningly at the beggar, who said, "Have you a paper to *give* me?"

This roused Jacob. "To give you?" he asked. "I sell papers!"

The beggar shook his head. "I don't buy papers. I beg papers."

"I sell papers," Jacob said again. "But if you need money to buy one, I can help you." He held out a coin.

The beggar shook his head again. "I beg papers. I was told you would have a paper to give me."

Jacob looked at the beggar, who waited indifferently. After a time, he took a paper from the top of a stack and handed it to the beggar. The tall man received it without thanks and began reading.

"What's this?" he cried suddenly. "Are you trying to cheat me? This is not today's paper!"

"I never sell old papers!" Jacob seemed very concerned. "Let me see it."

The beggar stepped back, shaking his head firmly. He was so near the packing box that Sir Stefan could read the paper in his hands. It was a copy of the *Times*. He could not see the date, only an item on the back page: "Ferry wrecked in the Philippines."

"It's my paper," the beggar said. "Look at your own papers. This one is for three days from now!" He rustled it impatiently and began to read again. "Mostly about Christmas celebrations," he complained. "You'd think nothing else happened." He turned to an inner page. "City news: disturbances in Times Square. How our brave police saved the city from malicious rowdy elements. Only ten lines. They must want to sweep it under the carpet." He read on. "Other things are to be swept under the carpet too. 'Sad death of a well-known figure in Times Square.'" He shook his head approvingly. "They handled this one well."

"Is it anyone I know?" Jacob asked. "Let me see." But the beggar stepped back farther. Jacob began to look through the rest of his papers, all of which seemed to be of this day's date.

The tall beggar folded the paper, ripped it to pieces in his strong hands, and threw the fragments in the air. They scattered over the square. Sir Stefan reached out for one that landed near him, but found only snow. "Imagine!" the beggar laughed, "a newsdealer asking for a paper! A newsdealer should have all the news, and even some personal messages, shouldn't he?"

"Yes," the puzzled Jacob admitted at last. "Even some personal messages."

The beggar winked. "I have such a message for you."

"From which person?" Jacob asked eagerly.

"From a fat old gentleman."

"Oh." Jacob seemed disappointed. Then he asked, "What was the message?"

"More accurately, a report," the hawk-faced beggar replied. "Since he has been immersed in the milieu of the performing arts, he finds it appropriate to present his report in the form of a theatrical review." The beggar drew a sheet of paper from within his long coat and fixed a broken pair of spectacles to his nose. He read: " 'This reviewer considers the evening's performance of historical rather than intrinsic interest. The choreography was superficially attractive. There were elements of suspense; nor were irony and pathos lacking. However, the events themselves were tangential and predictable, even banal. The commercial spirit was omnipresent. Violent episodes that provided a contrast were overlaid by a bourgeois drabness. They do not bear comparison with similar past and future events. The night's happenings, if they are recorded at all, will become part of the dull social history of—without meaning offense—a dull land!'

"In short," the beggar said, "he was not impressed." He swung his spectacles between thumb and forefinger. "From his remarks to me, I learned that the gentleman did not find the lightness, the freedom of spirit, the *élan* he was led to expect. He will go to a place where 'the soldiers don't make the old men dance.' He was much taken with the phrase when you used it some time ago to describe America."

A terrible suspicion rose in Jacob's mind. "And did all this"—he swept his hand around the square—"did all this happen just to show how wrong I was?"

"Who can say? Don't underestimate your own importance. As for the phrase about soldiers and old men: 'all this' is nothing. For other words and phrases great cities fall, fires blaze round stakes, skulls are piled high!" Then the beggar coughed apologetically. "But I'm waxing rhetorical again. It's a fault I still haven't shaken."

Jacob sighed. "So, he will go away."

"*They* will go away," the beggar replied. "He and his clients, the dancers."

"The dancers must go?"

"Indeed, yes," said the hawk-faced beggar. "They are too innocent to remain alone on earth: they might be corrupted."

Jacob said bitterly, "That never seemed to worry anyone before."

"Before, they couldn't see as well as they can now."

"But they can't stay?"

"No," the beggar said, "that would be impossible. Two of them are not enough to protect each other."

Slowly Jacob said, "Two are not enough. Would three be enough?"

The beggar winked. "Please note that it was you, not I, who asked this. I can only say that it is not entirely impossible that three could support each other sufficiently. No further comment on this point is permitted."

Then the beggar tossed his glasses over his shoulder and jauntily walked away. Somehow, a walking stick had appeared in his hand, and he swished the snowy surface of Broadway as if it were a field of flowers.

In the next few minutes, snow blotted out all footprints; soon the square resembled a snowy meadow in the old country. Across this space, Sergeant O'Toole came riding on Fergus. The horse walked heavily as if he too were saddened by the evening's events. The sergeant had not taken part in the police action. He was suspected of unreliability when firmness was called for in dealing with the criminal element; plans for the night's cleaning-up raid had not even been mentioned to him. But he drooped, as if he had done it all.

A black cape, hem trailing in the snow, moved swiftly across the square from 45th Street. It was Sergeant O'Toole's friend, the dancer. She seized Fergus's bridle, swinging him around just in front of the newsstand. "Oh, I found you!" Her voice was husky with emotion. "I waited at the theatre. I knew you'd pass here again!" The sergeant sat bemused, his face suddenly pale. "We're going away," the dancer said. "Did you know we're going away?"

"Yes, I knew," the sergeant said.

"Why didn't you come to the theatre? Why didn't you?" the dancer looked up at the tall sergeant. Her voice softened. "I guessed you wouldn't come to look for me, so I had to look for you." She shrugged back her cape and looked up at the sergeant. "But you *will* write me, won't you? I'll write you from the road."

"Of course I'll write you, miss," Sergeant O'Toole said.

"Don't call me that!" Then the dancer shook her head and added, to take away any harsh impression, "You policemen are slow! But we have time."

The sergeant climbed stiffly down from his horse. "I thought our time was all over."

"Never say that!" the dancer cried. "You know I'll be back."

"But you have your career," the sergeant said dutifully, without much conviction.

"Indeed I do," his pretty friend responded. "But how long does a dancer's career last? Not nearly so long as a policeman's. I'll be back." She turned her head. "They're calling me now; we leave tonight." She stood on tiptoe and kissed Sergeant O'Toole on the cheek. "Wait till I'm back," she whispered.

As she glided back toward the Xanadu Theatre, where a row of taxis waited, the sergeant stood still, rubbing his cheek with one gloved hand. Then he took off the glove to touch his bare hand to his cheek. Fergus stood motionless, following the dancer with great shining eyes.

11

&

And now Grandfather, who had been looking anxiously at Mr. Eisbein, insisted that he rest again. For the last few minutes the guitars across the river had been strumming. Before Mr. Eisbein could argue, the clear voice of the girl singer announced, "Our next song, the last one before the break, will be an old Basque folk song, about a boy whose sweetheart was so bright that she couldn't live in the village where she was born. He followed her from the village to the great city, and at last to the kingdom itself. If you listen to the melody, the meaning of the words may reach you too."

Then they sang in the beautiful Basque language, and soon both Grandfather and Mr. Eisbein dozed off. They slept till the song, a long one, ended; then both awoke at the same time. Mr. Eisbein yawned, rubbed his eyes, and, in an easy, cheerful voice, continued the story.

Sir Stefan could see Sergeant O'Toole on Fergus's back patrolling thoughtfully up and down 7th Avenue. The wind had dropped now; snowflakes stayed where they fell. The tall policeman became whiter and whiter, while the horse's warm black skin melted the flakes that touched him.

Something thumped on the newsstand. Sir Stefan poked his head out through the blanket and saw that the two dancers were there with their mannequin, which they had casually leaned against a corner of the newsstand; in a minute it resembled a snowy bunch of sticks.

Sir Stefan heard, in the silence, Jacob's rapid breathing. At last the girl dancer said, "Did you see how the sergeant's young lady slipped across the square? That gliding step! She might almost have been skating on the snow. Anyone can see that she's a dancer."

"Will they marry?" Jacob asked. "Will they be happy together?"

"We can't tell you," Simon answered quickly.

Esther added, "At present we aren't permitted to tell you such things."

"At present?"

"In your present condition."

Jacob shook his head. "I'm in good health."

"I'm glad," Esther said, "though you do look worn."

"Well," said Simon indignantly, "what do you expect?"

"Yes," Jacob admitted, "I have been under a strain. During the last few days, I often felt as if I were dreaming. Perhaps I was; I hope not." He looked at the dancers. "But I'm explaining myself badly."

Esther said, "We understand you. After all, we too once had dreams."

"We did," said Simon. "I dreamed I lay in a filthy barracks, surrounded by the smell of vodka and onions, and peasants with dull, harsh voices. Rats ran over my feet. I dreamed that someone had told me, as a joke, that a plague had struck our village, so I must be glad I was safe. In my dream, someone else said, 'Your kind always gets out of trouble.' "

"That was a terrible dream," Esther said. "But we had kinder ones, even though they were foolish. Once we dreamed that our words could change history; that in our state, as it was then, we could change events by a single magic word."

Esther looked behind her. A late hansom cab, driving uptown, was approaching silently. Directly before it, a chilled, numb pigeon huddled in the snow. Esther said, "Frangipani." The pigeon made an effort, fluttered up, and escaped just before the cab's wheels could pass over it.

"So, now you know both the magic word and the right place to use it," Jacob said.

Esther shrugged. "Yes."

"How happy that must make you!"

"Not especially," Esther said. Jacob stared at her. "You see," she continued, "for a good deed here, a bad deed there. If we bring good luck to any creature, elsewhere another one will suffer."

Simon added, "That pigeon was saved. But another one will die that would have escaped. Mr. Spangler explained it to us; he said the balance, the moral balance, of the universe must be maintained."

Jacob looked at his friends with pity. "But how sad for you to have such powers and not use them."

"Not so sad," Simon answered. "We really have no more power than before, but now we know how weak we are."

"How terrible it was, not to know!" Esther exclaimed. "Once we only dreamed, as you are doing now."

"But when we awoke," Simon said enthusiastically, "how clearly we saw!" Then his voice choked back as if he had said more than he should.

The snow had slackened to a flake or two, but now a sudden shower fell. "Poor Jacob," Esther said, "all your papers will be covered. You look like a snowman already."

Jacob started to close his shutters, but this blocked his view of the dancers; he opened them wide again. "I heard you will go away," he said very quietly.

Neither one answered him at first. Then Esther sighed, "We think so."

"I wish you could stay," Jacob said.

"That isn't in our hands," Esther replied.

"Will you go to another city? Another part of America? Perhaps your Mr. Spangler will take you to the West, where the air is clean and free," Jacob said hopefully. "I thought of moving there myself."

"Much farther than that, Jacob," said Simon. "We think, to other worlds."

Esther said, "Out of the solar system, out of this galaxy, even out of our universe. So far that you can hardly tell one star from another, they say; so far that you can certainly not tell one person on Earth from another."

"*They* say," Simon added, "that from such a distance each inhabitant of the Earth will appear as exactly alike as atoms of one kind. But *we* think that isn't so, Jacob."

Esther said, "From whatever distance, we think we will be able to identify a certain newsstand in New York City, and its inhabitant."

All fell silent again. "I wish you could stay," Jacob said again.

"Do you *really* wish it, Jacob?" Esther asked him.

The silence that followed this question was broken in a few minutes by a curious hissing sound, then a splutter. "My kerosene heater must be out of fuel," Jacob said, distracted. "Still, my light bulb gives some heat."

"You should go home," Simon said.

Jacob asked, "Will you be here again in the morning?" Neither dancer replied. "I'll leave soon," Jacob said.

A new gust of north wind veered off the opposite side of the square and struck directly into the newsstand. Jacob started to close the shutters again. "But now I can't see you," he said. "I don't want to lose sight of you."

"You really should go home," Simon insisted.

Jacob said to Esther, shyly, "Perhaps *you* could come into the newsstand for a bit."

"Gladly," the girl replied. "But I'll give you no warmth."

"It will seem warm," Jacob said.

He closed the shutters completely. Simon called, "Jacob, you'll be so cold!"

"Not really," Jacob's muffled voice replied, "I won't stay long."

The newsstand door on the side opposite Sir Stefan's box opened and closed. Simon walked away, sadly, toward the Times Building. Sir Stefan saw him walking up and down beside the stout man, who kept his hands behind his back and stared up at the surrounding buildings as if nothing that was happening at a lower level concerned him.

Only a thin shaft of light came through the newsstand's shutters, its line on the snow broken as one or another of the occupants passed before the light bulb. "What did Simon mean when he said how clearly you could see when you woke up?" Jacob's voice asked.

Esther's voice said, "Oh, we can see very clearly indeed now. We can see birds in the sky, much farther away than you could. We can even see birds hidden in clouds, and at the same time see the clouds around them."

"Yes?" Jacob said eagerly.

Esther's voice continued: "We can see veins in leaves of grass, worms in the earth, and right down inside worms, if we choose; even the movement of the fluid they use for blood. We can see fish in the water, and the pattern of their scales. If we choose, we can see the blood circulating in their fins and gills."

("Why are you wiggling?" Grandfather asked Paul. "Don't get impatient at this stage of the story." "I wasn't impatient," Paul said.)

Esther said, "But truly, Jacob, you should go home. I can see it's growing colder here, from your face."

"Does my face show that?" Jacob asked. "I hadn't noticed. But you were always good at reading faces. You could even read what I thought."

"*That* was nothing!" Esther replied. "Now we can truly see into people's thoughts: not only the conscious ones, anybody could do that, but also the thoughts that are there without the owner knowing it."

After a time, Jacob asked, "Did I have such thoughts, too?"

"What shall I tell you, Jacob?" Esther asked. "You never hid

114

what was on your mind. What a simple and open person you always were!"

"But the thoughts beneath?" Jacob persisted. "Was I always thinking then as I am now?"

"Ever since you came to America, we watched your hidden thoughts grow. Some day, we thought, you might decide to join us. We hardly dared hope it. It grieved us — but we missed you so!"

"Yes, I always loved you," Jacob said.

Then the voices inside the newsstand became so low that Sir Stefan couldn't make out the words. The pair inside continued to whisper together.

And soon, Sir Stefan fell asleep. He told me he had a dream, too (Mr. Eisbein said). He dreamed of a seagull frozen in the ice that tried hard to escape. Finally, only the wings flew away, leaving the rest of the bird behind, looking very surprised and comical.

Sir Stefan awoke in his warm, cozy nest to hear the newsstand door open. In a moment, the girl dancer emerged and walked toward the Times Building, where her brother waited. But she stopped halfway there and looked back. At the corner of the newsstand the mannequin stood up by itself and began dusting away the snow. With a feeble step, which grew stronger and stronger, it walked toward the girl dancer, who took its arm until they had joined her brother.

Sir Stefan puzzled at this till he fell asleep again. It was daylight when he awoke, to the sound of heavy blows. Two pairs of blue legs stood before his box. He cowered back, and looked through a peephole in the side. The police were knocking on the newsstand's shutter, where the light inside had made them suspicious.

Sir Stefan could see the two dancers, and the third one, standing by the Times Building. He spotted the stout man too, sitting very high up on a ledge of the building, rubbing his hands together. As a policeman thrust his nightstick between the newsstand's shutters and, with a great *crack!*, pried them open, the three dancers departed, quietly walking down Broadway. The stout man, his legs stuck out like those of a child on a fence, continued to watch the show beneath him.

12

Aᴺd suddenly, Mr. Eisbein stopped talking. Paul waited for him to continue. "What happened then?" he finally asked.

"What happened? Why, the police broke up the newsstand."

"But what did they find inside?"

"What should be inside? Newspapers and the like."

"Where was Uncle Jacob?"

"Where should he be? He was gone."

Paul looked at Mr. Eisbein, then at Grandfather. "He wasn't there anymore?"

"No, you could say he wasn't there anymore."

"Come on!" Paul said. *Really?*"

"Well," Mr. Eisbein said. Then, after another long silence, he added. "I talk too much. At my age we run on; we don't know when to stop." Mr. Eisbein turned his head toward the Home. "Here's your mother," he said in a relieved voice.

Paul saw his mother and Aunt Bessie waving to them. But as they started to walk toward the bench, he sat still, watching Mr. Eisbein, who was completely silent.

"My goodness, you're all so quiet and serious," Aunt Bessie said. "Are you waiting for the river to talk to you?"

"Something like that," Grandfather said.

"Were you worried, darling?" Paul's mother asked him. "I left a message on the desk." Paul looked at her without speaking. "Did they tell you, Papa?" his mother asked Grandfather. "Bessie just had to go to this other auction. I called the desk again to give them the number, in case they had to reach us. Did they tell you?"

"I'm sure they will," Grandfather said. He asked Aunt Bessie, "How was the auction?"

"I bought rocking horses, Papa," Aunt Bessie said. "A gold one and a silver one."

"Rocking horses?" Grandfather asked. "Toys?"

"They're antiques now. They're beautiful, Papa. I only had room for one in my wagon. I'll get the second one the day after tomorrow. I'll bring it to show you."

"Will you?" Grandfather asked happily. He and Aunt Bessie were fond of each other, even if they often quarreled about politics. Aunt Bessie called him "Papa," though, as Aunt Sophie had pointed out, she didn't have as much right to do so as even Paul's mother, who had married his son.

Paul still hadn't spoken. "Where's your sweater?" his mother said. "In the Home? Why didn't you remember to put it on? I bet you're sniffly." She reached for his forehead to feel his temperature, but Paul dodged away.

Aunt Bessie put a hand on Grandfather's shoulder. "Papa, we have to go now," she said. "Sarah doesn't want us to be on the road after dark. Don't you want to go in yourself, and rest?"

"I'm not tired," Grandfather said.

"Maybe a little? Your friend, too?" Aunt Bessie smiled at Mr. Eisbein. "You should both rest."

"After our walk. We haven't had our walk yet," Grandfather said.

Aunt Bessie looked at him. "Yes, after your walk." She turned her attention to her nephew, "Time to go, Paul," she said. "You'll come back soon. Sarah," she said to her sister, "why don't you find his sweater? I'll get him to the car."

When the others were gone, Grandfather and Mr. Eisbein took their usual walk along the river, back and forth between the apartment houses. The singers in the bandstand were back with a new act. One played, the other two danced: ballroom dances, tangos, waltzes, swirling peasant dances. The two men danced elbow to elbow, bobbing because of their unequal heights. The voices of barkers rose everywhere: "Hit the target and drown the tramp!" "See the giant bearded lady, the ugliest person alive!" "Take a chance: what do you have to lose?"

"So," Grandfather said at last, "Jacob froze to death in his newsstand."

"That's right. The police found his body there."

"You didn't want to tell the boy?"

Mr. Eisbein shook his head. "I couldn't; something held me back. Besides," he added, "you saw how his eyes lit up as we talked of his great-uncle. I didn't want to describe Jacob's body. It was very light. He hadn't eaten much in the past week. The police told me this; the papers didn't mention it."

"Yes," said Grandfather. "I remember the newspaper story."

"In the *Times*," said Mr. Eisbein. "The day after Christmas. 'Sad death of a well-known figure in Times Square." And on the back page of the same paper, a column about a ferry wreck in the Philippines."

Grandfather nodded. "They showed me that notice after the funeral. I was out of town on business when Jacob died. My brothers Aaron and Reuben arranged for the funeral; for any other member of the family they would have wired me to come back in time.

"My brothers told me only a few of the family came to the funeral. They didn't want to discuss it; they were ashamed. They were probably convinced that Jacob was drunk when he froze to death, that he had starved himself, as alcoholics do. My brothers' wives must have heard rumors about the people Jacob had been associating with. They were whispering about dancers and even women of the streets. I didn't press for more details."

"I'll bet they didn't want to discuss it!" Mr. Eisbein said. They had reached one end of their promenade; as they turned back, he added, "There were more people at that funeral than they admitted to you. I was there, for one."

"No, they didn't tell me that. I'm glad you went."

119

"In fact," Mr. Eisbein said, "I arrived in a limousine."

"A limousine!"

"Not my own, of course. I came with the maître d' from Rector's restaurant, Monsieur Vladimir, a tall, austere man who had been fond of Jacob. His boss let him go, but wanted him back in a hurry. Outside the restaurant we found Felix, the former blind beggar, carving a model of the empty newsstand. He came with us."

Grandfather said, "I heard about a tall man in a limousine, who my brothers thought was a detective. They told me there was a policeman too. My brothers were sure they had come to check up on Jacob's associates, like the F.B.I. does at a gangster's funeral. Was that Sergeant O'Toole?"

"No," said Mr. Eisbein, "he was on duty. It was, of all people, Constable Tertis. He was hiding in the back of the memorial chapel when we arrived, touching his *yarmulke* suspiciously. He said, 'I had a dream that I should come here.' He wouldn't say any more.

"For the eulogy," Mr. Eisbein said, "the rabbi did the best he could with what the family told him. He said, this man, Jacob, like all his family, came to America to find a new life. He was a modest man, not so successful as his brothers. But in his work he had been respected; now he was mourned by his family. This he said doubtfully, as I remember; he shook his head at the few family members who were there; the funeral parlor had to supply some of the pallbearers. He said, if only this man had been spared! He would have achieved a success to make his family proud. More important, he would have married, have left descendants.

"And while he spoke, more people kept arriving. The rabbi cheered up, but not your family. Your brothers looked worried, as each stranger came into the chapel."

"They did talk about that," Grandfather said. "Reuben's wife said, 'What was it, a circus? At least they didn't come to speak to us!' "

"I can tell you who came," Mr. Eisbein said. "The wardrobe mistress from the Xanadu Theatre brought red roses, the kind they give to the star after a performance. Usually such roses last for three shows, but these were new. She also brought a wreath with white carnations on behalf of one of the dancers, Sergeant O'Toole's friend, now on the road. Four minor actors, still with greasepaint from playing soldiers in *Anthony and Cleopatra* at the Knickerbocker Theatre, added a certain military air.

"Two streetcar lines crossed just by the chapel door. Each car brought new people, who joined the procession from the chapel to the cemetery, just two blocks away. It was on Long Island; you could still see the Sound then. The new mourners, mostly traveling salesmen, kept sniffing the sea air, cold as it was.

"I saw Tannenbaum, the one who had the dream. For once in his life he had left his case of crucifixes behind. Hermann Bleiweiss, a candy salesman, who remembered Jacob from his candy-store days, came in his wheelchair. Usually his son, a promising salesman in his own right, pushed him; now he was pushed by Gonzalo, the hot-chestnut vendor. He seemed more comfortable pushing something; I had never seen him otherwise.

"And there were more," Mr. Eisbein said. "I stopped at the cemetery gates to watch them all. The family came first, with the coffin bouncing on the pallbearers' shoulders. M. Vladimir led the rest of the mourners, with old Bleiweiss rolling up at the end. I waited to keep him company.

"But when we gathered round the grave, we saw there might be still other visitors. A cart came in sight, an old peddler's cart; and the fat driver, with a cloth cap, his broad trousers tucked into his boots, a regular Tevye the Dairyman. Except for the words 'Eggs, butter, hens' on the side the cart might have come from the old country.

"As it went along the fence, I saw it had other occupants: a little orchestra. A short man with an accordion, a taller man with a flute, and a girl with a mandolin."

"Yes, I remember," Grandfather said. "Reuben's wife said they even brought music to the graveside."

"She exaggerated," said Mr. Eisbein. "The musicians stayed outside the cemetery. And they played quiet songs, no words; but most of us knew them; songs about fields and oak trees, and soldiers who go to the wars. Many of the mourners cried again."

"I think the family held that music against Jacob more than anything else," Grandfather said. "Though even *they* couldn't have imagined he had anything to do with it."

"No," Mr. Eisbein agreed. "They couldn't have imagined that."

The old men turned and started back over their path. "Three musicians in the cart," Grandfather said thoughtfully. "That's not the only time that my family has been bothered by three musicians."

"They came back again?"

"It must have been them. There was the strike at Reuben's paint factory. The turning point was these three people who set up a coffee stand and sang for the picket line. This gave the strikers just the courage they needed to get a good deal. Reuben blamed everything on those three: he was sure they were sent direct from Moscow. I'll have to tell Bessie about them. She'd appreciate that story."

"I think so too," Mr. Eisbein said. "She's a fine girl. A pity I'm so old."

"And the testimonial dinner for my brother Aaron," Grandfather continued, "after he built the social hall at the synagogue. A three-piece band was supposed to provide light music for dancing afterward. Instead, the members sang a song about a modest rag-and-bone man, a small-time junk dealer, who liked to repair broken objects, make them useful again, and sell them at a modest profit. Aaron turned red, his mouth became all sour. The song was about his own life, of course, before he became such a big dealer in scrap metal. He used to boast that he had broken up more ships than were in the Spanish Armada. He certainly didn't want to be reminded of his early life or of the past when he bothered to mend things."

Mr. Eisbein smiled happily.

Grandfather's voice became softer. "They may have been involved in a much happier incident, too. It was my brother David's daughter, Jenny — she couldn't have a child, one miscarriage after another. She was growing desperate. She was a nervous little thing; a child meant everything to her, and she was now in her mid-thirties, almost too old to have one. Her husband was as bad as she was; when she became pregnant again, he watched her with panic in his eyes. They put her in a private nursing home near Woodstock, for complete rest. But she wouldn't settle down. The crickets in the woods terrified her, she imagined field mice were coming in through the windows. There were signs that she'd lose this baby too.

"Then these three singers came up from the village and sang outside the nursing home almost every evening. She forgot herself, forgot the child even, in listening to them and waiting for them to come. The singers were there too the night the child was born, a son."

"What became of him?"

"He's a professor of astronomy now, very famous. A couple of years ago, Jenny phoned everyone from Chicago, where she lives, to say he would be on television. I saw him speak. Brilliant! He uses all the telescopes and fancy equipment, of course, but someone talking about him afterward said he seemed to have the stars and their motions and laws inside his own head as well. I think I'll write Jenny," Grandfather added. "She could come for a visit. She might remember what song they sang."

The red rim of the setting sun winked at them from above a row of apartment buildings to the left of the fairground. The air grew chilly. "We'd better go in," Grandfather said to Mr. Eisbein. "How's your heart?"

"Okay. Still working."

"I didn't like the way you looked earlier."

Mr. Eisbein agreed. "It's more excitement than I'm used to."

"Well, take it easy."

"Don't tell me. Tell them!" Mr. Eisbein nodded across the river. In the bandstand the three musicians danced to a recording of the "Winter" section of Vivaldi's *The Seasons*. A spotlight shone on the bandstand, so that the dancers were much brighter than the crowd below. The girl's red skirt whirled and beckoned.

"I think they'll take it easy now," Grandfather said. "What

more could they get from us? We've told the story." The two old men were silent for a few moments.

"Enough for tonight," Grandfather said. "Let's go in."

13

Paul's mother was still worried about his catching cold. Before they started, she reached to the back of the station wagon and pulled a blanket for Paul off the rocking horse. The horse was almost four feet long, dappled gold and white. "Isn't he a beauty?" Aunt Bessie exclaimed, as if she were seeing it for the first time. "Wait till you see his brother. We had to stay till the end of the sale to bid on them."

Paul looked at the horse again. The deepest gold was in the pupil of its eyes which, by some trick of the light, seemed to wink at him.

"We should have left the auction sooner," his mother said. "Paul was out in the cold all afternoon. He never stayed so long before."

Aunt Bessie said, "Your mother was worried you'd be bored, or your grandpa would be bored, or something."

"Not bored," Paul's mother said. "Tired. I thought he might ask too many questions. And Papa is so forgetful."

Paul stared at his mother. "Not always forgetful," Aunt Bessie said.

"He often forgets," Paul's mother insisted. "Sometimes I

have to remind him of people he once knew. Even members of his own family."

"He was remembering today," Paul said. "He sure remembered a lot!" Then he added, incautiously, "I think he had some help."

"Help?" Aunt Bessie asked.

"You mean Mr. Eisbein," his mother said.

Paul hadn't, but he decided he had better not tell his mother, or even Aunt Bessie, just who he thought had been helping. He nodded, neutrally.

"Well, you don't necessarily want to believe everything Mr. Eisbein says," Paul's mother told him.

Aunt Bessie looked at Paul in the mirror. "But what did your grandpa remember that you found so interesting?"

"It was about Uncle Jacob and his friends," Paul said.

"At last!" his mother exclaimed. "He's been asking everyone about this great-uncle. You know" — she whispered to Aunt Bessie, but Paul heard her — "the one they don't like to talk about; the failure."

"And what did they tell you?" Aunt Bessie asked Paul.

Paul wanted to think about the story for himself right now, not to share it even with Aunt Bessie. But he had to say something. "He had these friends in the old country, in Poland. After he went to America, they came over for him." Then Paul added, "He died."

His mother drew in her breath. "Did your grandfather tell you that?" Paul shook his head. "Mr. Eisbein then, did he tell you?"

"No," Paul said. "He didn't want to."

Aunt Bessie asked dryly, "Do you think this Jacob is still alive, Sarah?"

"He might be."

"If he were, we'd have heard of him by now, surely?"

"Not necessarily," Paul's mother said. "You know what the family is like. They don't talk about certain things."

"Oh, I know!" Then Aunt Bessie asked Paul, "Who were these friends of Jacob?" After a while she asked, "Cat got your tongue?"

Paul muttered, "They were a man and woman. They were dancers."

"Dancers!" his mother said. "He went off with a couple of dancers. No wonder they don't talk about him."

Aunt Bessie had to keep her eyes on the road but, quickly, they questioned Paul in the mirror. "It doesn't sound like a suitable story for a child," his mother said. "I'll have something to say to that Mr. Eisbein!" She told Paul, "So you can't be sure he's dead at all, darling. Probably he's still with his dancers."

"I think he is," Paul said.

A little later, when they stopped in a shopping center, Paul's mother insisted that he stay in the car. Aunt Bessie stayed with him. "Don't let him brood," his mother whispered to her. "Sometimes he thinks about things for *days!*"

But Aunt Bessie let Paul think about things for some time. Finally, he felt her watching him and turned his head. "That must have been quite a story," Aunt Bessie said. "I know you don't want to talk about it now." Paul did not contradict her. "Maybe later." She looked at the shopping center entrance, through which her sister might emerge at any moment, and smiled. "Just one question: these 'friends' of your Uncle Jacob, the dancers, what were they like?"

"They could see everything!" Paul said. "They understood everything that happened."

"They sound very wise," Aunt Bessie said. "Were they involved in any kind of political action?"

"Oh no," Paul said. "They knew they couldn't change anything."

Aunt Bessie seemed disappointed. "Well, we all have our own heroes. My heroine was Rosa Luxemburg, the great revolutionary who was killed by the fascists. I wanted to be like her, except for being killed so young. Your heroes seem to have had better luck." Aunt Bessie saw the doubtful look in Paul's eyes. "Did you *like* them, Uncle Jacob and his friends?"

Paul thought some more. "Yes, I did."

"Was the girl beautiful?" Aunt Bessie asked. "Did your Uncle Jacob go off with a dancing girl? No, that's not the story?

127

Oh, I can see you like them; they attract you. But do you want to *be* like them? Why, what's the matter?''

For Paul's face had twisted mightily. He gasped; tears ran down into his open mouth. "No!" he sobbed. "I'd rather be alive!"

Aunt Bessie opened the door, came into the back seat and put her arms around him. "But you are alive, darling; very much alive! Did they frighten you, your grandpa and his friend?"

Paul shook his head violently. When he could control his voice, he said, "They were all so lonely: they wanted to have their story told!"

"Hush," said Aunt Bessie. "Hush. You can talk about it after." And she hugged Paul until he stopped crying. He was getting ready to talk to Aunt Bessie again, when his mother returned, put her hand through the window and touched his forehead. "I told you he had a fever!" she said.

Paul did have a fever, which was higher the next day and kept him in bed for a week. His mother blamed Grandfather and Mr. Eisbein. He heard her saying over the telephone down the hall that they had kept him out in the cold, that they had upset him with all that folklore about his great-uncle: no wonder he got sick!

But Paul knew better. In his fever, he saw faces on the bedroom wall, heard obscure songs and strange music. When his temperature was normal again, he realized that none of these had been real and that the fever must have started, without his noticing it, during that day by the river. This would account for all he had felt, and thought he had observed: the day's very clear light; the singers and their songs, which had seemed to speak directly to him; the fish he could see, even in the dirty water; the blood vessels in the snake, and even the molecules! He remembered now that he had just started to read about molecules in his Wonders of Science books a few weeks before, and that he had been very excited. So, naturally, when his fever made him imagine things, he imagined such things as these.

When Aunt Bessie came to see him while he was sick, she

purposely didn't bring up their last conversation. He was becoming properly ashamed of his silly emotional outburst that made him cry over the imaginary people in the story. The fever must have been responsible for that too. He was grateful to her for not mentioning it. Later, when he visited Aunt Bessie's house again, they talked of many things, but never of the day before his fever.

For some time, too, Paul stopped visiting the Home. When he saw Grandfather at his own house or at family gatherings, neither of them spoke of his Great-Uncle Jacob. When Paul began to go to the Home again, Grandfather's dresser was moved so that all the old photographs were hidden. You could only see them by going into the corner, which Paul never did. He saw little of Mr. Eisbein during these visits. Once or twice, Grandfather took him to say hello to his roommate in the sun room, where Mr. Eisbein sat playing cards with Mrs. Dobin, a quizzical expression on his face.

And as Paul grew older he put the whole day by the river, and the whole story, out of his mind. He forgot it completely. It was as if it had never happened.

But, of course, he had plenty of other things to think about. He read more and more, especially mathematics and physics, until his eyes blurred and he needed glasses. While still in high school, he took evening classes in biology at a nearby junior college. He only took time off from all these studies for swimming lessons, and he became a strong swimmer. He justified the time spent by telling himself that swimming was a healthful exercise; also, though the thought made him uneasy and embarrassed at his own vanity, that he must not drown, or he would not be able to pass on all that he had learned.

Grandfather died when Paul was in his first year of graduate studies in molecular biology at Yale. He went to New York for the funeral, which took place in a crowded cemetery in Long Island. Other services were going on at the same time. The family was shocked to hear guitar music and a few voices singing at one such service, which was hidden from them by large ugly monuments. Paul recognized Mr. Eisbein, whom he had not seen for years, bent over and weeping by his friend's grave. The very old man clutched Paul's arm; later, Paul drove him back to the Home, which gave Mr. Eisbein a chance to relieve his spirit by talking of Grandfather.

While doing so, Mr. Eisbein began to recall some of the things they had said, on a day when they sat by the river and Paul became sick. For some reason, Mr. Eisbein spoke especially of the conversation between himself and Grandfather when Paul had gone into the Home for his pills, and after he had left. Paul listened out of kindness at first, then was surprised to find that these conversations, reported out of context, still made sense to him. Dimly, he began to recall other parts of the story, which he had not forgotten as completely as he had thought.

But just then he had to study for some very important examinations and to begin his research project. These occupied his mind fully; he had no time for more fanciful thoughts.

While visiting New York at the end of the summer, Paul learned that Mr. Eisbein had died the week before. Mr. Eisbein, who had not recovered from Grandfather's death, had insisted on walking alone by the river in the evenings. When he was late for supper one night, Mrs. Dobin set out in search and found him, quiet at last, smiling on the bench that looked toward the empty fairgrounds.

That afternoon, Paul was strolling by the lake in Central Park thinking mainly of his research which — not to be technical — concerned the role of protein molecules in cell membranes. In his mind's eye he could almost see how the molecules were fitted into the membrane, and how they moved. These concepts occupied him entirely, until he looked up for relief at the lively crowd round the lake. There were many performers: magicians, flame-swallowers, steel bands, and jugglers. There was even a preacher with a sharp Yiddish accent, a man in a long black coat with a sharp pointed black beard that he thrust out aggressively between sentences. He was preaching, of all things, about the Book of Job in the Bible: the story of a good man who suffered terrible misfortunes because of a casual bet between God and Satan. But the preacher had lost his way in the text and his words made no sense at all. None of his few listeners even bothered to laugh.

Three guitarists, one a short man with a kind, twisted face, sang a ballad which, Paul found, made a pleasant background to his own mental processes. Their song, what he heard of it, concerned a lazy messenger who stopped at the tavern, at the workshop, at the library, everywhere: so that the message was not delivered. The chorus, always sung by the girl of the trio, ran:

> "Oh, the foolish messenger:
> He'll wander about forever!"

Paul wandered on, his mind turned back to his molecular model. But a cry from the preacher arrested him. The song must have brought the preacher's sermon in focus because, with little preamble, he began talking of the messenger who had given Job the terrible news that all his sons were dead. "The messenger said, 'And I only am escaped alone to tell thee!' " cried the preacher. He raised a finger. "But suppose he had *not* escaped? Or suppose he had escaped and not told? He wouldn't be in the Book! It would be as if he had never existed!"

The preacher thrust out his beard fiercely. Then, as if struck by the sense of his own words, he let his mouth fall wide open. Paul could see his red gullet shining between his black beard and his mustache.

The three musicians, who had fallen silent during the preacher's words, began to applaud. Paul walked past them, but the female singer, a strong, rosy girl in a blue shirt and faded jeans, addressed him. "Aren't you going to hear our song? We've come such a long way to sing it!"

Paul shook his head and walked on quickly. In a moment, he realized he had been needlessly rude and turned back. But the singers, and the preacher too, had disappeared in the crowd. Though he searched for them, they were quite gone.

So Paul did not hear the song then. Perhaps someday, he thought, he would hear it. In any case, he really did not have time to worry about the matter then.

But the story he heard that day by the river has entered his mind more and more clearly. Its details, and how it was told, have piled up so that his head scarcely has room for them, let alone for his real work. Sometimes, when he closes his eyes, he sees a bench by a river and two old men, sitting on either side of a small curly-haired boy, all staring across the river at a fairground. And sometimes, whether his eyes are closed or open, it seems to him that he could reach out his hand and touch the story or the storytellers.

Recently, Paul has been wondering if he himself should write down the story, of which he is now the sole possessor. He may do this very soon: partly, to clear it from his mind, at least for a time; mainly, because he thinks that if he does not do so Uncle Jacob and his friends will come back one day and make him tell it again.